Hart's Last Stand

CHERYL BIGGS

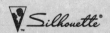

Silhouette®

INTIMATE MOMENTS™

Published by Silhouette Books

America's Publisher of Contemporary Romance

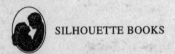

SILHOUETTE BOOKS

ISBN 0-373-27143-3

HART'S LAST STAND

Copyright © 2001 by Cheryl Biggs

This edition published by arrangement with Harlequin Books S.A.

® and TM are trademarks of Harlequin Books S.A., used under license. Trademarks indicated with ® are registered in the United States Patent and Trademark Office, the Canadian Trade Marks Office and in other countries.

Visit Silhouette at www.eHarlequin.com

Printed in U.S.A.

Desire and anger, resentment and need.

He'd lived with them all for a long time, enduring and ignoring them, but now they were stronger than ever.

Part of him wanted nothing more than to ignore everything that had happened in the past and just drag Suzanne into his arms and take what he'd always wanted, to taste, finally, the sweetness of her lips against his, to feel the slender length of her body pressed against him and experience the passion he knew slept deep within her.

How many nights had he lain in bed unable to sleep, his thoughts all on her, almost feeling her body next to his, wondering where she was, what she was doing, who she was with.

Some nights he'd felt as if his memories were slowly killing him. Other nights he'd wished they would.

He'd thought that was all behind him, that his feelings for her were dead. Now he knew he'd been wrong.

ROMANCE

Dear Reader,

Once again, we've rounded up six exciting romances to keep you reading all month, starting with the latest installment in Marilyn Pappano's HEARTBREAK CANYON miniseries. *The Sheriff's Surrender* is a reunion romance with lots of suspense, lots of passion—lots of *emotion*—to keep you turning the pages. Don't miss it.

And for all of you who've gotten hooked on A YEAR OF LOVING DANGEROUSLY, we've got *The Way We Wed*. Pat Warren does a great job telling this tale of a secret marriage between two SPEAR agents who couldn't be more different—or more right for each other. Merline Lovelace is back with *Twice in a Lifetime*, the latest saga in MEN OF THE BAR H. How she keeps coming up with such fabulous books, I'll never know—but I *do* know we're all glad she does. Return to the WIDE OPEN SPACES of Alberta, Canada, with Judith Duncan in *If Wishes Were Horses....* This is the kind of book that will have you tied up in emotional knots, so keep the tissues handy. Cheryl Biggs returns with *Hart's Last Stand,* a suspenseful romance that will keep you turning the pages at a furious clip. Finally, don't miss the debut of a fine new voice, Wendy Rosnau. *A Younger Woman* is one of those irresistible stories, and it's bound to establish her as a reader favorite right out of the starting gate.

Enjoy them all, then come back next month for more of the best and most exciting romance reading around—only in Silhouette Intimate Moments.

Yours,

Leslie J. Wainger
Executive Senior Editor

Please address questions and book requests to:
Silhouette Reader Service
U.S.: 3010 Walden Ave., P.O. Box 1325, Buffalo, NY 14269
Canadian: P.O. Box 609, Fort Erie, Ont. L2A 5X3

Books by Cheryl Biggs

Silhouette Intimate Moments

The Return of the Cowboy #762
The Cowboy She Never Forgot #911
Remembering Jake #953
Hart's Last Stand #1073

CHERYL BIGGS

was never really a reader while growing up, but got hooked on gothics, then romances, when her three children were little. While they napped, she read. Finally she decided to write a romance. That manuscript went into the closet, with the next four or five. Years later, after selling her personnel agency, she pulled out her first manuscript and went to an RWA conference, which garnered her an agent and several good friends. A year later that first book was sold, and a dream came true.

Cheryl lives in the San Francisco Bay Area, in a sunny suburb at the foot of Mount Diablo with her husband, five cats and a blue-eyed dog. Her children are now grown, and in her spare time she loves to travel, shop, read and try to talk her husband, Jack, into adopting just one more animal.

This book is dedicated to my own Cobra Corps hero,
my husband, Jack, who lent me his expertise
on the military and Cobra, and was always there for me
when I needed encouragement.

Chapter 1

The plane's engine coughed again and the nose propeller stopped.

"N299V, wrong runway. Repeat. *Wrong runway!*"

Suzanne Cassidy glanced at the radio, bit her lower lip and tightened her grip on the control handle. She was out of fuel and out of time. She couldn't correct.

Suddenly six black Cobra helicopters began to descend in front of her.

She shrieked, and instinctively pulled back on the handle and closed her eyes.

The plane jerked, the nose lifted briefly and the wheels hit the ground, hard.

Suzanne was slammed back against her seat. Her eyes flew open and she fought the control handle as the Cobras abruptly veered off. The new Cirrus

SR20 she and her partner had just purchased for the
company skidded down the runway.

Suzanne cursed and applied the brake harder.

The plane slid sideways and off the pavement, its
wheels grinding through grass and dirt.

Rocks pinged off the undercarriage.

The right ring wheel plunged into a shallow gully,
and the Cirrus came to a jarring stop.

Somewhere in the distance a siren began to wail.

Suzanne ignored it and struggled to catch her
breath. Her heart was slamming against her rib cage,
her hands were shaking and she felt weak all over.
Nevertheless she threw the door open and scrambled
out onto the wing.

"Lady, what the hell did you think you were doing back there? This is a military base, not a flight
school. You could have gotten us all killed."

She spun around at the deep voice as she slid to
the ground, then half leaned into the wing, half
clutched it for fear her legs would not hold her up.

The six Cobras sat on the runway a short distance
away, their rotor blades still slicing the air, but Suzanne paid them little heed. It was the man approaching that riveted her gaze. Panic seized her.

She wasn't ready to face him yet. Not like this.

Get back in the plane and fly away, a voice in the
far reaches of her head screamed. *Now!*

Instead, she stood frozen, unable to move or even
breathe as she watched him close the distance between them. Suzanne realized the moment he recognized her, and she felt her insides roil as her
nerves threatened to get the better of her. It had been
almost a year since she'd left Three Hills, but not
one day had passed that she hadn't thought about

him and wondered what might have happened between them if Rick hadn't been killed.

Memories tried to crowd in on her, bringing darkness and pain with them, but she pushed them away. There was no time for that now, not if she wanted to survive.

"Suzanne."

Her name sounded ripped from his lips, like an ugly curse he hadn't wanted to utter but was unable to restrain.

The hot afternoon sun turned the dark-blond strands of his hair to burnished gold and glinted off the aviator-style sunglasses, which reflected an image of the chopper hangar behind them, the desert surrounding it, even herself, but obscured his eyes. Suzanne didn't need to see his eyes, however. She remembered them vividly. They were the darkest, deepest blue she'd ever seen, like the desert sky during a summer storm. Dark, turbulent and dangerous, and always, it had seemed, beckoning to her.

She felt a tremor shimmer through her body and tried to look away. Instead, her gaze skipped over his long, lean body, its well-honed length complemented by his military flight suit. Her eyes darted back to his face, moving slowly over rough-hewn features that could never be termed classically handsome.

Nevertheless, he was striking, devastatingly so.

Friend...or enemy? The question that had been playing over and over in her mind for hours sent a chill racing up her spine as she looked at him. Someone was trying to destroy her, maybe even kill her, and Hart Branson was either the only one who could save her...or the one responsible.

She had come to find out which.

Without another word, without even waiting for her to respond, Hart spun on his heel and stalked across the tarmac toward an open hangar.

Startled, Suzanne watched him walk away, then shook herself, grabbed her bag and followed. She may have been a fool for coming to him, may have put herself in more danger, but she couldn't give up. Or let him refuse her. There was no one else to turn to, nowhere else to go. "Hart, please, just listen...."

He jerked around. "What do you want, Suzanne?"

She stopped and stared at him, momentarily taken back by the hostility she sensed, not only in his tone, but in his entire being. It seemed to radiate from him like the heat from the runway.

Why? The question pounded at her. What had she ever done to make him so angry with her?

The need to escape his hard, probing stare nearly overwhelmed her.

Get back in the plane and leave, the voice of her own fear said again.

She resisted giving in to it. "The...the FBI came to my house."

Hart didn't move, and his features seemed set in stone.

She swallowed, hard, and forced herself to go on even though she could almost feel his disdain pushing her away. "They said military secrets were stolen during Rick's last mission."

When he didn't respond, Suzanne went on, "For some reason they kept the theft quiet, but now the secrets are being sold and they...they..."

The air above the tarmac shimmered beneath the

merciless Arizona sun, but his silence was chilling, and stoked her already frayed nerves.

"They insist Rick's alive, Hart."

She heard the thread of hysteria in her voice, felt the sting of panic-driven tears behind her eyes, fought both and hurried on. "They think he faked his death, that he stole the secrets and sold them and that I'm his accomplice."

Fury ignited within Hart instantly, threatening to explode and tear him apart, and only by force of will was he able to control it.

He'd been betrayed before and he would most likely be betrayed again, but he would never believe that of Rick, and she knew it. So why had Suzanne really come back? What did she really want? He had never expected to see her again, and that had been just fine—more than fine—because as far as he was concerned, it was her fault Rick Cassidy was dead.

Turning abruptly, he tore off the dark glasses, walked into the hangar and threw his helmet and flight board onto a workbench, then spun back to face her again. "Do you really expect me to believe this, Suzanne?"

She'd followed him inside, but now she stopped. His disdain and rejection were too much, a lethal jab at the fear she'd been trying for days to deny she even felt. Tears sprang to her eyes, hot and burning, threatening to spill over. Every cell in her body trembled with desperation.

With concentrated effort she threw back her shoulders, stiffened her spine and searched for strength as she blinked rapidly in an effort to hold back the tears. "It's the truth." She'd meant it as a hard, convincing statement. Instead, the words came out as little more than a shaky whisper.

Hart stared at her, his eyes narrowed, distrust scorching hotly through his veins. Every woman he'd let become a part of his life, every single one, had cheated and lied: first his mother, then his only aunt, foster mothers and even his ex-wife. But Suzanne's transgression had been the worst of all, because hers had gotten a man killed.

He'd learned early in life that a man who trusted anyone but himself was a fool. To trust a woman was even worse.

And every time he'd ignored that lesson, he'd ended up sorry.

He turned back to the workbench and reached for the coffeepot that sat on it, his fingers forming a fist around the pot's handle and squeezing mercilessly as his anger deepened.

A year ago Suzanne Cassidy had been the wife of his best friend, the only real friend Hart had ever had, ever allowed himself to have. In spite of that, he had found himself attracted to her the moment they met. He'd loathed himself for it and tried to banish the feelings by sheer will.

He remembered one night when Suzanne had shown up to say goodbye to Rick just minutes before they were to ship out on an unexpected mission. It was when Hart watched her kiss Rick and tell him to be careful that he'd known he cared about her too much. One hell of a wake-up call for a man who didn't believe in love or giving his trust or anything else of himself to anyone.

He'd requested a transfer the same day they'd returned to the base. Out of sight, out of mind, he'd figured. But the transfer had been denied.

Then Rick had been killed and Hart blamed Suzanne, because he knew she'd done the unforgivable.

So why did he suddenly feel an almost irresistible urge to drag her into his arms and claim her lips with his?

Self-loathing filled him.

Why did desire simmer within him, threaten to burst free and consume him, overwhelm him, when he looked at her now—even when he considered her little better than a murderer?

He set the coffeepot down with a crash, too angry to be aware of the hot liquid that splashed on his hand. He turned back toward her. "Rick was no traitor, Suzanne."

Sunlight streamed through the window behind him and touched her tears, turning them to tiny shimmering reflections of the sun's rays.

Hart drew on his anger to steel himself against the compassion the sight stirred in him, but he couldn't stop his eyes from drinking in her beauty, or his senses from appreciating it. Delicacy and strength were both evident in the face he'd always found far more alluring than any other woman's. As he studied her now, he realized she had grown even more beautiful than his memories of her.

Suzanne's lips were a blend of perfect curves and tempting fullness that beckoned his own. Her nose was slightly turned up at the end, giving her an air of sassiness, while the deep brown of her eyes, splintered by tiny chips of gold, held the richness of the desert floor on a moonless night.

His gaze moved over the pale-yellow silk blouse she wore, lingered on the curve of her breasts, the narrow breadth of her waist, subtle curve of her hips and the way her jeans held snugly to her long legs.

Suddenly all the old feelings crowded in on him. His fingers ached to slip within the silky darkness of her hair, to slide through the waves that cascaded over her shoulders, to wrap around the nape of her neck and pull her toward him, to caress her curvaceous body, to stoke her passion until...

He clenched his hands into fists as the traitorous emotions soared through his body. What was the matter with him? He didn't want to feel these things.

"I know Rick wasn't a traitor," she said finally, breaking the cold silence that had settled between them. "But what I'm telling you is the truth. As unbelievable as it sounds, Hart, I swear it's true, and I need help. I thought..." Her voice broke, but she forced herself to go on. "I thought...maybe you could...maybe if you would..." She couldn't finish.

The hostility that emanated from him, the anger she felt fill the space that separated them as he glared at her were too much. He hated her.

The realization shocked Suzanne.

He hated her.

It was so obvious now. But why? She didn't know...and yet it really didn't matter. Hope fled from her heart as completely and swiftly as a deer flees a hunter.

She turned toward the door, nearly knocking over a stool in her haste to escape him as panic started to overwhelm her. She'd been a fool to come here. To think he'd help. Her tears burst free, blinding her and turning the world into little more than a blurry collage of color. She stumbled, then paused, wiping at her eyes in an effort to bring her surroundings into focus, to turn the sunlight streaming through the open hangar door into more than just an undefinable bright blur.

Guilt and regret instantly rushed through Hart, but he fought them off as staunchly as he did the urge to reach out and stop her. Tears were just one of a woman's many tools, and most women knew how to use them all too effectively. Another lesson he'd learned a long time ago—repeatedly.

He moved to stand beside a disabled UH-60 Blackhawk, leaning his back against the gunner's door. Yet in spite of the lazy appearance of his stance, every muscle in his body was taut, every nerve on end. He couldn't give her the benefit of the doubt, or even consider believing her. It was out of the question.

Nevertheless he was curious and wanted to know more.

"So if I assume your story is true, why come to me, Suzanne? What do you expect me to do?" He tried to keep his features as hard and unrelenting as he tried to keep his voice. Part of him wanted her to walk out of the hangar without answering. But another part of him, the part he had to fight off with everything in him, urged him to close the distance between them, pull her into his embrace and take what he'd wanted, what he'd dreamed about for so long, and damn the guilt, the world and everything else.

Suzanne turned and, as their eyes met, felt her breath nearly desert her.

For the briefest of seconds she saw desire flame

to life in his eyes, felt it reach out to her, beckon to
her and stoke the fires of the attraction she'd felt for
him before Rick's death.

Then, as abruptly as the glimmer of desire had
appeared in his eyes, it was gone, and there was
nothing left there but cold anger again.

Flushed, her mind refused to collate an answer to
his question. She looked away again, suddenly engulfed by a flash of memories: the first time she'd
met Hart...the attraction that had stirred within
her...the guilt that had followed. It hadn't mattered
to Suzanne that her marriage was virtually over, that
her husband had indulged in numerous affairs, that
she had been the only one still trying to make the
marriage work. The guilt had eaten at her night and
day, relentlessly.

Her mother, who fell in love as effortlessly as
most people fall asleep, was on her sixth husband,
and Suzanne had always been determined not to follow in her footsteps. For richer or poorer, in sickness
or health, until death do us part—that had been a
promise she'd intended to keep, no matter what.

Then Rick had demanded a divorce.

She pushed the memories aside and looked back
at Hart. How well had she really known him? He'd
been Rick's senior officer and friend, not hers. Had
she been a fool for coming to him?

Friend or enemy? The words echoed through her
mind again, taunting her as she stared at him. Yet
in spite of them and the fear that gripped her, that
undefinable something that had been between them
since the day they'd first met, still drew her to him.

Suzanne stiffened against the sensations assault-
ing her. For the past year she'd been building a bar-

ricade around her heart, protecting herself, and now she could feel the structure weakening and threatening to crumble.

Her emotions were in turmoil only because she was so scared, that was all. A month ago the FBI had shown up at her door and questioned her relentlessly. Last week after their third visit, she'd known she had to do something to stop their badgering questions and prove their suspicions wrong. She'd called her cousin Molly, a State Department employee and the only person she could trust. But Molly hadn't been at work or home. She was on a survival trip somewhere in the wilds of Montana, and according to both her boss and her mother, she was totally unreachable.

That was when Suzanne had known the only person who could help her was the only person who'd seen Rick die—Hart.

She felt his gaze on her and pulled herself together enough to answer his questions. "I came to you because I don't have anyone else to turn to. I don't want to end up dead or spend the rest of my life in prison, and to avoid that I need your help, Hart."

She watched his eyes narrow again, his jaw clench tightly and the small vein on the side of his neck twitch ever so slightly. Apprehension seized her. A shiver of fear skipped up her spine and swept goose bumps across her skin.

Oh, God, she prayed, *don't let him be the one I should be running from.*

Reason and rationale warred with the resentment and anger that had been pent-up inside Hart since Rick's death. Her claims were ludicrous. Too ridiculous to be anything but impossible. Even so, they could explain why someone was investigating him.

He mulled the possibility over in his mind, trying to look at it rationally and calmly.

A week ago his company commander had informed him that someone from Washington had called and asked some very pointed questions. That wasn't unusual. Someone was always asking questions about the Cobra Corps, even though just about every assignment the army's elite, special-ops helicopter unit was given was top secret.

It was still a fairly new unit, as far as the army was concerned, having been borne out of a special mission during the Persian Gulf war. Six men brought together to fly a mission most others considered suicidal. But they'd succeeded. Now the Cobra Corps, attached to the 12th Aviation Brigade, 99th Cavalry Division Air Mobile, consisted of thirty-two men, all pilots and officers, with a special attachment of mechanics, aides, communications officer, crew chiefs and a medic. Their permanent base was Three Hills, Arizona, but they could be called out at any time for anything. Their missions were usually classified and highly dangerous; rescuing political hostages, "relieving" certain political pressures, circumventing political uprisings, dealing with the before, or aftermath, of terrorists, and conducting top secret surveillance, being the usual types of assignments.

But this time the questions had been about Hart. Still, neither he nor the company commander had been overly concerned. Hart was the corps's flight leader, and he was up for promotion. The questioning wasn't routine, but someone was probably just being overly efficient, ordering a check on him "for the record." A formality.

But he should have been concerned, because yesterday someone from Washington, and he didn't know who, had requested his 201 file. To request an officer's personnel file from his commanding officer was an unusual request. It could mean nothing; someone had a question about him before approving his promotion, or he was being considered for a special assignment and his background was being rechecked. There were numerous possibilities, including that his career was in serious jeopardy.

Now he wondered if these incidents and Suzanne's sudden return and unbelievable claims could be connected?

He shook his head. He was letting his imagination run wild. Anyway, his commanding officer had denied the request. No one had gotten his file.

Hart caught Suzanne's gaze and held it mercilessly. "The feds can't resurrect a dead man, Suzanne."

Bitterness tinged his tone.

"Hart, I don't—"

"Rick *is* dead, Suzanne. I saw his chopper take a direct hit. I saw it explode and go down in a shower of flames and debris. No one could have survived that."

She took a step toward him, panic rising in her again. Whether he was out to destroy her or he was her only chance to survive, she couldn't allow him to send her away. She wouldn't. At least not until she knew the truth and could prove it.

Make friends with your enemies, Rick had once said. *It throws them off guard.*

She stared into Hart's eyes, searching for answers to questions she never in a million years would have imagined herself asking. But that was before the FBI had come knocking on her door.

Had Hart murdered Rick to protect himself? Was he the man the FBI should be considering a traitor? Maybe even a murderer? She took a deep breath. Was it really possible the body they'd identified as her husband hadn't been Rick at all? She had to get Hart to help her and in the process convince herself he was innocent, or find some way to prove he was the one setting her up.

"The FBI doesn't believe Rick's dead." She pulled a file folder from her bag and, hands shaking so badly she nearly dropped it, tossed the folder, open, onto a mechanics table near where Hart stood.

He looked down at the papers suddenly scattered atop the table's tools, but didn't understand what he was supposed to see.

"That's a copy of a bank statement for an account I never knew I had," she said, pointing to one.

He looked down at the statement. It was a new account, opened only six weeks ago. His gaze moved to the bottom of the page, and he noted the balance: $155,000.

She pointed at a photograph that lay beside the bank statement. "And that's a picture of me talking to a man the FBI claims is a European spy."

His gaze moved to the photo, recognizing Suzanne but not the man she was talking to. He looked back at her, still unwilling to believe, even for a moment, that anything she was saying could be true.

She could have deposited the money herself and be lying to him now, and the man in the photograph could be anyone. Her accomplice—a friend, a lover, even a stranger she stopped on the street. But why would she make up such an elaborate lie? What did she really want?

"He came into the auction house where I work..." She paused, realizing Hart didn't know she'd revamped her career. "I don't teach school anymore," she said. "I'm a partner in an antiques auction house and gallery in Beverly Hills now." She paused again, momentarily distracted by thoughts of just how much her life had changed since the last time she'd seen Hart.

She'd gone to Los Angeles with every intention of continuing her career as a high-school teacher. But two days into her new job several students in one of her classes started arguing and she couldn't get them to stop. A moment later the sound of gunfire exploded in the room, and one of the teenagers fell to the floor.

She'd taken a leave of absence from her job, too shaken to even think of returning to her classroom. A week later she'd been browsing through a little shop that sold all sorts of bric-a-brac when she had run into Clyde, who'd been talking with the owner. Clyde Weller was Suzanne's second cousin on her father's side and had been her best friend through high school. They'd lost touch over the years, but seeing him again proved to be just what she'd needed.

They'd gone to dinner and talked, and talked and talked and talked. Finally, well into the wee hours, Clyde made a suggestion that seemed so natural Suzanne said yes instantly. She was widowed, had received a large settlement after Rick's death she needed to invest, and her degree was in history, with art as her minor. Clyde had been doing freelance bidding on antiques for others for years, so he was already well connected in the business and had always planned on opening his own gallery/auction house.

It was as if fate had brought them together again. They'd pooled their resources, as well as their last names, and started Casswell's.

Hart stared, but didn't question her, so she decided not to explain. He obviously wasn't interested in her personal life, which was fine. She only needed his help in clearing herself of the FBI's ridiculous allegations.

"Anyway, about two months ago this man in the picture came into the gallery and introduced himself as Mason Brunswick," Suzanne continued, "and said he was thinking of consigning Casswell's— that's the name of our business—some very old paintings for auction. The next day, on my way home, I ran into him on the street. We chatted a minute, and he asked me a question about one of the paintings. That's obviously when the photo was taken."

"So again, assuming this story of yours is true," Hart said, "and somehow Rick survived that crash—and the body identified as his wasn't, what do you think I can do?" He didn't even know why he was asking. Her story obviously wasn't true. It had taken six months after the Jaguar Loop mission and Rick's memorial service before the army had been able to recover his body. But they *had* finally recovered it, and he *was* dead. So what did Suzanne really want? What could she possibly hope to gain by these ridiculous claims?

He didn't know.

Nevertheless he knew that, instead of asking questions that had kept her from leaving, he should have just gathered up her so-called evidence, handed it back to her and sent her on her way.

"You're the only one who saw Rick die," Suzanne said, seeing the cynicism that still shadowed his eyes. "Hart, you saw it happen. You're the only one who can swear that it was Rick who got in the Cobra that day, that it was Rick flying it, that Rick is dead—if he really is."

He didn't answer.

She continued to meet his hard stare as doubt and suspicion assailed her. What if she'd just walked into a trap? What if he'd cunningly drawn her into it and she was doing exactly as he wanted? What if he was the only person on earth who could help her, but wouldn't believe her? A torrent of *what if*s slammed her. She felt all her senses and feelings intensify: fear, attraction, suspicion, longing.

Her heart raced as he looked at her for several very long, very tense moments. His scrutiny made her breathing become ragged and forced, the blood rushing through her veins in a tumultuous, speeding, hot flow that made her light-headed. She'd known confronting him would be difficult, maybe one of the most difficult things she'd ever done, but it was proving far harder, far more complicated than she'd ever imagined.

Say something, she silently demanded, and gripped one hand with the other upon realizing they were trembling. *Control,* she told herself. She had

to keep herself under control and not break down.
She tried to pull her gaze from his, needing to escape those penetrating eyes, and found it impossible.

A chill swept up her back, then rippled through
her entire body. *Say something,* she silently pleaded
again. But it wasn't only his silence that unnerved
her, or even the cold fear that had invaded her
senses. It was the urge she felt to reach across the
space that separated them, to touch him and feel his
warmth, his strength. The feeling was almost more
than she could resist.

How many times since she'd left Three Hills had
she thought of him? Dreamed of him? And told herself to forget him? To put all thoughts, all memories,
all fantasies about Hart away?

She curled her fingers into fists and held them
rigid at her sides, trying to force away the feelings
she knew could only prove her downfall.

"The FBI is building a case against me, Hart."
Her voice sounded weak and pleading, but she
couldn't help it. "They obviously believe Rick survived that crash—or that it wasn't him flying the
plane that day."

She inhaled deeply.

"My only chance to prove this so-called evidence
they have against me and Rick wrong is you."

"They retrieved the body," Hart snapped. "They
identified it as Rick. You want to believe they were
wrong?"

She looked at him and shrugged. "The FBI
does." He saw the fear and desperation she was
fighting to hide and the tears she was struggling to
hold back.

Hart fought to control the emotions warring

within him since the moment she'd turned from her plane and he'd recognized her. Desire and anger, resentment and need. He'd lived with them all for a long time, enduring them, but now they were hotter, stronger than ever.

Part of him wanted nothing more than to ignore everything that had happened in the past and just drag her into his arms to take what he'd always wanted, to taste, finally, the sweetness of her lips, to feel the slender length of her body pressed against him and to experience, revel in, the passion he knew slept deep within her.

How many nights since she'd left Three Hills had he lain in bed unable to sleep, his thoughts all on her, almost feeling her body next to his, wondering where she was, what she was doing, who she was with?

Some nights he'd felt as if his memories were slowly killing him. Other nights he'd wished they would.

But he hadn't dreamed about her now for at least a month. He'd thought that was all behind him, that his feelings for her were dead. Now he knew he'd been wrong.

But what he was feeling wasn't all memories and nostalgia, or even desire, because he also wanted to slam a fist through something and frighten her into telling him the truth. He wanted to grab her, jerk her to her feet and demand she stop lying.

"Hart, please," Suzanne said. "You have to listen. I…"

He shook his head and strode past her to the door. "Rick's dead, Suzanne. You know it, I know it, the army knows it, and I have no doubt the damned FBI, if they have any reason to want to—knows it, too."

Chapter 2

"May I help you, miss?" The aide looked up from the file cabinet he'd been rifling through.

"Yes, I…" Suzanne glanced at the door to Hart's office. She knew he was in there. Listening. Nerves, fear and desperation skittered through her veins. "I…I'd like to see Captain Branson, please."

"Let me see if he's available," the private said. "Your name, miss?"

"Suzanne Cassidy." Why didn't he just come to the door? He surely could hear her.

The aide closed the file drawer, turned and disappeared into Hart's office, closing the door behind him.

A moment later he returned, but instead of saying anything to her, he merely nodded and walked directly to the exit and left.

She looked back toward Hart's office and felt a start of surprise. He was standing in the doorway, leaning one shoulder against the doorjamb. Sunlight, streaming in through his office windows, shone at his back, turning his hair to a golden halo and creating myriad shadows about his face.

Suzanne tried to stop staring, ordered herself to look elsewhere and couldn't.

"Suzanne," he said, breaking the silence between them and the spell that seemed to have dropped over her.

"I…" Her throat was suddenly as dry as the desert, and her fingers were wrapped around the strap of her bag so tightly she realized her nails were pushing painfully into her palms. "I have no one else to turn to, Hart," she said finally, retrieving at least a small part of her senses.

He straightened.

She felt an involuntary start of alarm, but forced herself to remain still. He was an old friend and he was a stranger. She needed him and she feared him.

Strength exuded from every line of his body, hardness shone in his eyes. Fine lines radiated from the outer corners of his eyes and bracketed his mouth, but Suzanne knew Hart was not a man who laughed easily or frequently.

She also knew that, in spite of needing his help, there was no way she could afford to trust anything he said.

"There's nothing I can do for you, Suzanne," Hart said, stiffening. He couldn't let her back into his life, he thought coldly. He wouldn't.

She watched him walk across the room, jerk the exit door open, and for just a moment look back at her, his eyes cold, wary and full of anger. Seconds later, as she ran after Hart, she heard someone call out to her.

"Suzanne?" the corps crew chief said. "Suzanne Cassidy?"

She stopped and looked at him. Everything about him was thick—his neck, chest, waist, arms, even his hands—while his eyes were a dull gray, nearly the same color as his hair, and his face was marred by a mass of craggy lines that reminded her of a metropolitan street map. "Chief Carger," Suzanne said.

For a while, just after she and Rick had moved to Three Hills, Rick had thrown Monday-night-football parties, and some of the other pilots, the crew chief and a few mechanics had come to the Cassidy bungalow to eat Rick's barbecued burgers and watch the game on television.

She remembered Rick telling her once that the chief had lost his family years ago in a house fire. The army had become his home since then, and the corps members his family.

At first she'd liked the chief, thought of him as a father figure, as the men did, and she and Rick had him over for dinner several times. But after a while something about him began to make her feel uneasy.

"Yes, ma'am. Nice of you to remember." He nodded. "Good to see you again." His gaze skipped over her quickly, and Suzanne suddenly remembered exactly what it had been that used to make her feel uneasy around him. "Hope everything's been going okay for you." He glanced at Hart. "Sorry, sir. If I'm intruding, I can—"

Hart hadn't missed the quick, but thoroughly assessing once-over the chief had given Suzanne. Before Rick's death Hart had suspected the chief had been more than a little interested in Suzanne, but he'd put it down to his own paranoid jealousy. Now he felt his hunch had probably been right. They'd both been attracted to their friend's wife.

"No, what is it, Chief?" Hart snapped, damning himself as much as the chief.

"Just wanted to let you know, sir, that we've got a problem with one of the birds. Cowboy's. Fuel line. May not be able to fix it for a couple of days, unless I can get the parts sooner."

Hart nodded. "Fine. Reb is on leave. Have Cowboy use his chopper if need be."

The chief nodded. "Yes, sir, that was my thought." He glanced at Suzanne again. "Suzanne—Mrs. Cassidy. Nice to see you, ma'am."

Suzanne waited until he'd left, then turned back to Hart. "Please, just consider—"

He averted his gaze. "No."

She fought back the feeling of fear and desperation that threatened to send her to her knees sobbing and pleading with him. Instead, she found a very thin, very fragile thread of composure and walked past him and down the path to the street.

A phone booth stood beside another building a few yards away. She stepped into it and began flipping the worn pages of the dilapidated directory that hung on a chain, searching the pages through a blur of tears. "He can't say no," she muttered softly. "He can't." She finally found a number for a cab company and dialed it on her cell phone.

Hart would think over what she'd said and help her, she told herself. He had to. There was no other way, nowhere else for her to turn.

* * *

Hart hung up the phone and threw down his pen.

All his commanding officer would say was that no one was investigating him because of his pending promotion. But someone *was* investigating him.

Instinct, and the fact that he'd never believed in coincidences, told him that whatever was going on was connected to Suzanne.

He reached for the phone and dialed a number he'd never thought he would need.

"Senator Trowtin, please," Hart said to the secretary who answered.

Three years ago terrorists had kidnapped Senator Keith Trowtin while he was on a goodwill mission in the Middle East. The CIA had tracked their movements and tried to rescue him three times. Four good men had died in the effort. Then they'd asked for the corps's help. The senator was being held in a desert camp, less than ten miles from U.S.-friendly territory. Hart's plan had been risky and dangerous, but no one had come up with anything better.

"Tell him it's Captain Hart Branson," he added.

The senator came on the line a moment later. "Captain, good to hear from you. I was just telling Julie—"

"Senator," Hart interrupted, deciding to spare no words, "I need a favor."

"I owe you my life, Captain."

"I was just doing my job, Senator."

"It was a suicide mission, Captain, and we both know it, but somehow you pulled it off and we're both still alive. So whatever you need, you got it. What is it?"

"Someone's investigating me, sir. I need to know who and why."

"I'll call you back."

Hart replaced the phone receiver and began to pace the length of the room, uncertain whether he felt better or not. He hated asking for favors. Before he could decide which way his mood was swinging, the phone rang.

"Evidently the feds suspect you of treason," the senator said.

Hart felt the breath stall in his lungs.

"And the word murder is also being bandied about."

"Murder?" Hart gasped, incredulous.

"Top-secret plans for an experimental weapons-detection device that was being tested during a covert operation you led a year ago were stolen during the mission, Captain, or right after it."

"Senator, you know I wouldn't—"

"You don't have to convince me, Captain, but you need to know—the feds have two theories. One is that either the pilot who went down in that chopper over there wasn't killed, his death was faked and the two of you are accomplices, along with his wife. Or, you and the man's wife conspired to steal the plans, killed him and she's now selling the plans through a Los Angeles gallery she's a partner in."

"This is unbelievable," Hart said. "I—"

"Listen, Captain," the senator said, "this could get ugly. If you need me again, call. I'll do what I can."

Hart heard a click and the line went dead.

It was worse than he'd thought.

He remembered everything Suzanne had said, the

fear in her eyes, the near panic in her voice. But was it real?

"Dammit to hell." He pounded a fist on his desk. His only chance to save his career now, possibly his life, was to prove both of them innocent—or the woman whose image had haunted his dreams for months guilty.

He stared out the window on the opposite wall and contemplated the situation. Rick was dead, which meant he was innocent. But what if Suzanne was not? What if she was a spy? What if she'd used Rick? Hart swore viciously. The whole damned thing sounded too farfetched, but in the world he lived in, it wasn't. She could be trying to set him up, could have come back not for his help, as she claimed, but to shift the blame.

He yanked the door open and stalked through his aide's office toward the exit. Turning to Private Roubechard, he ordered, "I want you to do a background check on Second Lieutenant Rick Cassidy. He served under me in the corps a year ago."

Hart paused, one hand on the exit's doorknob. "Do one on his wife, too. Suzanne Cassidy. And I want them on my desk in an hour."

The anger and resentment he'd lived with for the past year burned hot in him as he slammed out of the office and strode to his car. He slid behind the steering wheel and started the engine.

He didn't trust Suzanne, but he had to talk to her again.

It had seemed to take forever for the taxi to arrive. Suzanne was now halfway to Tucson when the sensation that she was being watched grew too strong to ignore. She turned and looked out the cab's rear window. The road behind was long, winding, narrow and very empty. Nevertheless, she was unable to shake the feeling or its intensity. She'd felt it on and off over the past several days, but now it seemed stronger than ever.

Her gaze swept the vast, open desert, and apprehension pulled on the knot in her stomach. She'd left Three Hills a little more than a year ago, and after settling in Los Angeles she had completely revamped her life.

But it hadn't stopped her from thinking about him.

She trembled as a wave of hot yearning swept through her. It raced up her spine, through her arms, legs and fingers as she remembered the moment she'd turned from the plane and faced him—the instant they'd recognized each other. She could still feel the piercing stare of his eyes, the potent essence of Hart Branson as it had reached out and enveloped her.

For the briefest of moments it had been as if his consciousness dove inside hers to probe her thoughts, uncover her secrets and search, then gently touch, her very soul.

He had never looked at her like that before. No man had.

Her cell phone rang, startling her and bringing her a glare in the rearview mirror from the cab driver. He hadn't relished driving to the base to pick her up, and it was obvious even the promise of a good tip hadn't improved his mood any.

Suzanne pulled the phone from her purse, hoping it was Hart telling her to come back, that he believed her. He'd help her. Then she realized it couldn't be him—he didn't know her cell number. Her spirits instantly plunged. Please, she prayed fervently, please don't let it be my mother. Not now. She wasn't in the mood to defend her reasons for moving to L.A. or hear why she should start looking for another husband, which seemed to be her mother's two favorite topics lately.

"Hello?" she said hesitantly.

"Suzanne, darling, what in heaven's name is going on? Are you all right? Where are you?"

She jerked the phone from her ear and nearly groaned aloud at hearing her partner's high-pitched, squeaky voice.

"I thought..." Clyde sucked in a breath. "Well, darling, when you didn't show up at the gallery this morning, I had the most awful visions, I mean..."

She shuddered, remembering her close call last night in L.A. She'd worked late at the gallery. The street had been deserted, but when she'd started to cross it, a car had suddenly appeared out of nowhere.

Only the fact that she'd realized she'd left her briefcase in the office and had started to turn around and go back had saved her.

Afterward she'd felt such panic that she'd driven straight to the airport. And the terror had prompted her to take their new plane at first light and fly to Three Hills.

"...you're never even late, let alone a no-show..."

"I'm sorry, Clyde."

"...and then Mr. Collins came in for your nine-o'clock appointment, and you weren't here, so naturally he was upset and..."

"I'm sorry," she said again, hoping she hadn't

lost the gallery one of their most valued customers. "I should have called you, but..." But what? She searched for an excuse, knowing she couldn't tell him the truth—for both their sakes.

"Yes, you've said that, thank you. So where are you?"

"Arizona," she said before she could stop herself.

"How did you...?" He gasped. "You took the plane?"

"Yes, I'm sorry, but there wasn't time to—"

"I know—you heard of a terribly wonderful find and just couldn't wait to get to it, right?" he said, offering her the best excuse she could ask for, even though his tone was somewhat sarcastic.

"I'm sorry, I should have called first, but—"

"Oh, never mind," he said, sounding placated at the thought of a handsome sale on whatever she'd gone to pick up that couldn't wait. "I handled Mr. Collins just fine, but I'll expect to see something deliciously valuable when you get back, so don't be gone long. And for heaven's sake, don't put a scratch on our new baby."

Her heart sank as she remembered their "new baby" sitting cock-eyed back at the military base, one wing wedged into the gully next to the runway. Rick had taught her how to fly during their first year of marriage, and she'd loved it, but she hadn't been behind the controls since his death. Guilt nibbled at her conscience. She was rusty and should never have taken the plane up. But she'd panicked.

The army had reluctantly agreed to rescue and stow the plane until she could make arrangements to leave. Of course they thought that meant tomorrow, but she had no intention of going anywhere until she felt safe again and knew the truth—and that all depended on Hart. He could save her. He was probably the only one who could.

Or he could be a cold-blooded killer, the dark side of her thoughts reminded her. He could have stolen the plans and killed Rick. He could be the one behind the FBI's suspicions, the one trying to frame her.

It made sense, and she didn't want it to.

The hair on the back of her neck suddenly seemed to stand on end. She jerked around, looked out the rear window again and nearly screamed.

A black Corvette was right on the taxi's tail, but the sun reflecting off the windshield made it impossible for Suzanne to make out the driver's face.

The car remained behind the taxi all the way into Tucson, and pulled in behind them at the entrance to the hotel where she'd made a reservation. Fear had settled in Suzanne's stomach like a boulder, heavy and immovable. She decided to wait until whoever it was in the other car stepped out, then she'd order the taxi driver to speed off and take her to another hotel.

The driver's door swung open.

Suzanne froze.

Hart pushed himself out of the Corvette and stood, his light-brown uniform molding to his body, accentuating length, complementing muscle.

Relief and something else, something she didn't want to feel for him, or even acknowledge, rushed through Suzanne's body like a flash flood. Compared to what her imagination had been raking up, he was the most beautiful sight she'd ever seen.

She quickly paid the cab driver and climbed out,

her legs shaking so badly she had to momentarily lean on the car door for support. "Hart," she said as he approached, "I didn't know that was you behind me. I thought—"

"We have to talk, Suzanne." He took her suitcase from the driver, grasped her upper arm firmly and steered her into the hotel and across the spaciously elegant lobby. "Get your room," he said curtly, "drop off your luggage and meet me in the coffee shop."

She nodded and approached the front desk, even though everything in her urged her to hang on to Hart for dear life. She was reluctant to leave his side because of the sense of safety she felt when with him, in spite of his obvious disbelief of her claims. But he'd come after her, and that was all that mattered now.

Once in her room she hurriedly slipped into a clean white blouse and a pair of sandals. Just before leaving to meet Hart, she drew back the curtain to the balcony to let sunshine pour in and warm the room. The view of the Arizona desert, sprawling out beyond the hotel for as far as the eye could see, was magnificent, and for a brief second she savored it, suddenly realizing how much she'd missed it. Then she saw a man standing on what appeared to be a path meandering through the foliage near the pool.

He was looking up at her.

Suzanne gave a start, her heart skipped a beat and she stepped quickly away from the window. Was he watching her? Or was she being paranoid?

A knock on her door sent her heart into her throat. "Suzanne."

She whirled around, her fear instantly abating as

she recognized Hart's voice. Just as instantly she admonished herself. She couldn't do that, couldn't put all her hope and trust in Hart Branson, no matter how much she wanted to. She had to remember to be wary of him, to suspect him of the worst. He could be the traitor. He could be a killer. He could even be the one who'd tried to run her down last night.

L.A. was only a short plane ride from Tucson. He could have been there. It was possible. She didn't want to believe that, but she knew men found it all too easy to betray a woman. It had been a lesson she'd learned the hard way, first from her father, then from a stepfather, a fiancé and finally from her husband.

She would never trust a man again, not with her heart, and especially not with her life.

Suzanne walked to the door and opened it.

Her gaze met his directly. In spite of the cold, ugly suspicions she was determined not to ignore or forget, a river of warmth swept through her as Hart's gaze met and held hers. "I thought we were meeting in the coffee shop," she said, surprised at how calm she sounded.

"I thought you might have changed your mind." He strode past her and into the room. "Maybe figured out that your lies weren't going to work."

Lies? Shock, then anger sped through her veins, burning away every molecule of caution and rationale, and dousing the desire that had been smoldering within her ever since the moment she'd stepped from her plane and saw him walking toward her.

She closed the door and turned, struggling to remain calm and resist the urge to stalk across the room and slap his face.

Anger gave her strength, and that allowed her to ignore her fears, at least for the moment. "I know what I've said sounds incredible, Hart, but I thought if anyone would or could believe me, it would you. You were Rick's best friend. But—" she shrugged and glared at him "—if you don't believe me, if you really think I lied, then I've obviously wasted your time and mine by coming here, and there's nothing left for us to talk about."

"Yes, there is." His eyes held hers, refusing to let her look away, forcing her to face the disdain and resentment he'd lived with for the past year.

Suzanne felt her breath nearly desert her, along with her anger. After a moment that seemed an eternity, she tore her gaze from his and moved toward a chair, twisting her hands together, then thought better of sitting down and paused beside the faux fireplace. It was only because she still found him physically attractive that her emotions were in such a tangle. She should have expected that.

"I made a few phone calls after you left my office earlier," he said, still standing in the center of the room.

She looked at him, wary again. Uncertain what to expect. "And?"

"Let's just say that I know there is *something* going on."

"Something," she repeated slowly. "But you don't believe what I told you?"

She saw the anger that flashed back into his eyes. "Rick is dead, Suzanne. He was the one flying his Cobra that day, not some doppelganger or science-lab clone. It was Rick, and there's no way he survived that crash.'' Hart shook his head. "No way. Which means there is absolutely no way he could have stolen those plans and be selling them now. And I'm pretty sure the feds aren't so stupid they'd believe that, anyway.''

"Then who?'' Suzanne asked, and added silently, *Other than you?*

He stared at her, and she suddenly realized that he suspected her. She felt her jaw drop, her hope shrivel and die. "You can't... No, I don't believe...'' She shook her head. "You can't really think I did it! How could I have stolen plans that were on that mission? I wasn't there.''

Hart's face remained a cold mask of scorn. "I don't know. But I know Rick didn't do it.''

She sagged against the fireplace. He wasn't going to help her prove her innocence. He was going to damn her. The prospect of actually being charged with treason, followed by a life in prison, loomed before her, bringing a chill to her veins and a terror into her heart like none she'd ever felt before.

"But what I think or even know at this point doesn't matter,'' Hart added, his tone as hard as the glint in his eyes.

Suzanne looked up in surprise, not understanding what he meant, but feeling an unreasonable spark of hope.

"They think I'm in on it with you.''

Shock rendered her nearly speechless. "What?''

He watched her closely, saw the disbelief and surprise that pulled at her features, but knew he couldn't believe everything he saw or heard. At least not yet, and especially not from her.

Suzanne sank onto a chair, her legs suddenly too weak to support her. The thought that the FBI would suspect him of being her accomplice had never crossed her mind. "Oh, Hart, I'm sorry. I never should have come to you. I never meant…"

To kill Rick? To get caught? To make me want you? The words screamed in Hart's mind, but not from his lips. "I ordered my aide to do a background investigation on Rick. I should have it by morning." He didn't mention that he'd ordered one on her, too.

She looked up at him, puzzled. "Why? You know Rick was a good soldier, and you said you saw his chopper go down. You said it exploded. You said no one—"

"I know what I said," Hart snapped, struggling to control his temper and hang on to at least a thread of patience. "But the feds don't believe he's dead, and I couldn't think of anywhere else to start."

Suzanne nodded.

"I'll go over the report in the morning, then decide what to do from there."

"I'd like to see it, too."

He frowned, instantly suspicious. "Why?"

She shook her head. "I don't know, really. I just know I have to be involved with whatever you're going to do about this mess. It's my fault you've been drawn into it. I shouldn't have come here."

He sat down in the chair across from her. *Play their game.* It was one of the first things he'd been taught in POW training. *Play your enemy's game and get inside their head.* It was a soldier's best chance of survival.

But he'd never lusted after any of his enemies.

He purposely softened his tone. "It wouldn't have mattered whether you came here or not," he said. "I was already being investigated."

"You were?" She frowned. Could she believe him or was it a lie to throw her off guard? "But why? By whom?"

He shook his head. "I don't know." He sat on the edge of his chair, arms resting on his thighs, and leaned slightly toward her. "Did Rick mention anything unusual to you the day before we left on that last mission?" He started to reach for her hand, then caught himself. "Think, Suzanne. It could be important. Did he say or do anything out of the ordinary?"

He demanded a divorce. She shook her head again. "No. Why?"

She was lying. He'd sensed it in her hesitation before answering, saw it in her eyes.

"I think something was bothering him that last day," Hart said.

She looked at him. How much did he really know?

Chapter 3

Hart paced the small sitting area of Suzanne's hotel room, struggling against his frustrations, against the resentment and anger that were roiling inside him and that he was trying not to let her see. He wasn't getting anywhere, and the longer they talked, the longer he looked into those fathomless brown eyes, the more he felt torn between ugly suspicion and the unfounded desire to believe her.

She set her glass of water on the coffee table, and he paused, turning at the sound of glass on glass. His dark gaze met hers, and for a split second he thought he saw the passion and mistrust he knew was most likely mirrored in his own eyes.

"I shouldn't have come back," she said again, though she wasn't really talking to him.

Hart slid a hand through his hair as he contemplated his next move. He knew how to play the game as well as anyone. Better, actually. And it was definitely time to play. He closed the distance between them and knelt in front of her. "Suzanne."

Innocence or treachery? Which was it that shone from those infinite depths, that coated her words, that hid behind that tantalizing smile?

He reached for her, and the moment his hand touched hers, and without warning, all the old feelings of desire welled up inside him, stronger than ever, a scorching inferno that instantly began to war with his suspicions of betrayal.

He'd meant the gesture merely as a way to get her confidence and trust. But it had been a mistake, one he had no doubt now would end up costing him dearly.

With an effort of concentration and training he pulled on the cold mantle he normally assumed when readying for a mission that would take him into battle—and possibly take his life—and shrugged the unwanted feelings of desire aside. He needed to stay focused. To remember that she was likely the most dangerous enemy he'd ever faced.

That caution might be all that stood between his life and his death.

"I'm sorry," he said softly. "I know you're scared, Suzanne, and I shouldn't have accused you of lying. It was a stupid thing to do. But you can understand, can't you? I mean, this whole thing sounds so unbelievable. I was taken back. I felt I had to test you."

He saw the wariness in her eyes. The fear. But was she afraid of him? Or afraid she wouldn't succeed in fooling him?

"Look, I'm sorry," he repeated, making an effort

to soften his voice further. "I know you have no reason to lie about something like this, Suzanne."

She looked down at the hand enveloping hers. "I didn't lie, Hart, but I shouldn't have come to you," she said. "Now they suspect you, too."

"I told you, someone was already investigating me. They requested my personnel file before you got here. I'm not quite sure where it fits, but your coming has added a piece to the puzzle and given me at least an idea about what's going on." That was probably the biggest lie he'd told in years.

She looked at him in surprise.

"It'll be all right," he said, seeing the fear still in her eyes, but not trusting himself, or her, to believe it was real. "We'll figure out what's going on."

Suzanne nodded. They'd been attracted to each other once, and the timing had been wrong. Terribly wrong. It was no better now, and she felt certain it never would be. Rick's ghost would always be between them.

Hart started to stand.

"No," she said quickly, surprising herself. She didn't want to be alone, didn't want him to leave for fear he might not come back. "Stay awhile longer, please. You were right, we need to talk. Maybe we can discuss this further over dinner."

And you'll tell me more lies? Hart wondered, still kneeling in front of her. Yet in spite of the ugly thought, he thought he saw innocence in her eyes. Or maybe it was merely the skill of a good actress. A well-trained spy, looking up at him guilelessly, letting him see what he wanted to see while she drew him into her deadly web.

And a good soldier knew when to confront his enemy and when to let them think he was coming around to their way of thinking, Hart reminded himself, and this was not the time for confrontation or assault. Congeniality was called for. Maybe even seduction. "I'd like that," he said, smiling at her for the first time since she'd returned.

Suzanne stole a glance across the table at Hart. Her reactions to him were intense. But she had to believe they were merely physical. She'd been so lonely since Rick's death. And in reality, long before that. But another whirlwind romance like the one she'd had with Rick before they got married was not what she was looking for. In fact, she wasn't looking for anything. Or anyone. She liked her life just the way it was. She was independent, successful, and...

Alone, a little voice in the back of her mind said.

She ignored it. The only reason she was here with Hart was that someone was trying to destroy her. She needed his help—that was all.

She opened her mouth to say something to him, but a movement near the entrance to the hotel dining room caught her eye, and as she turned, she instantly forgot every thought in her mind. The man she'd seen near the pool earlier looking up at her room stood talking with the maître d'.

He was short and wiry with small eyes, dark, oiled-back hair, dark complexion and a thin black mustache that followed the curve of his upper lip and ended bluntly at each corner. She thought instantly of a weasel. A very dapper, very slick and very polished weasel.

The maître d' motioned with his hand, and both

men began to cross the room toward Suzanne and Hart.

She stiffened.

The maître d' breezed past.

The man from the pool caught her eye.

A slight smile pulled at the corners of his mouth, and he nodded.

Suzanne cringed and instinctively pushed against the back of her seat. Was that his way of telling her she was being watched?

Hart saw Suzanne's reaction to the man passing their table. He glanced over her shoulder and watched as the man took a seat at another table. Was he Suzanne's accomplice? Or had she recognized a federal agent? Was that a warning to the man he'd seen in her eyes or fear of him?

"Who was that?" he asked, deciding his waning patience wasn't going to abide anything at the moment but a direct approach, even if all it garnered him was yet another of her lies.

"I don't know, but I saw him earlier. He was watching me."

"Watching you?" He nearly scoffed at what was most likely a lie, and his mind raced to figure out where to put this piece of the puzzle. Feigning concern, he leaned forward and lowered his voice. "Where was this, Suzanne? And when did you notice him watching you?"

"When I—"

"Excuse me, señorita."

They both looked up to see that the man in question had returned and was standing beside their table. He nodded to Hart, then looked back at Suzanne and smiled widely, but there seemed a sadness in his dark eyes that didn't disappear with the warm gesture of his lips.

Hart saw Suzanne's fingers tighten around the delicate stem of her water glass, but the move didn't completely obscure the fact that she was trembling. At least, it didn't obscure it from him.

Fright or nervousness? he wondered.

"Yes?" she said.

"Excuse me," the man repeated. "I am Salvatore DeBraggo." He offered a curt bow, at the same time scooping up Suzanne's free hand and raising it to his lips. "Are you not Señorita Cassidy from Casswell's Gallery in Beverly Hills, California?"

His accent was extremely thick, but Suzanne understood every word. Mainly because they'd brought her a rush of relief. She'd almost expected him to pull out a knife or gun. She smiled, feeling foolish. "Yes, I am, but I don't believe we've met, Mr...."

"Oh, no, señorita, we have not met. You see, I have been dealing with your associate, Señor Weller. I have a very extensive collection of antique jewelry, my late wife's, actually. But—" he waved a hand, as if in dismissal "—we had no children, so there is no one to give the jewels to and I could use the funds."

"I see," Suzanne said.

"Yes. I would like to place them up for auction, and when I spoke with Señor Weller today on the telephone and he realized you and I were both here in the same city, he assured me you could—"

Hart felt his temper rising. He was trying to handle the possibility of losing his career, deal with espionage, treason and betrayal, and keep his burning libido under control, and this overly polished dandy was trying to arrange an auction? The rein on his patience snapped.

"Look, Braggo," Hart interjected.

"Señor DeBraggo," the man politely corrected, still smiling but not taking his gaze off Suzanne.

"Señor DeBraggo," Hart repeated with more than a touch of sarcasm purposely instilled in his tone, "Ms. Cassidy is here on vacation, at least for the next few days, so if you wouldn't mind…"

The man handed Suzanne a card. "Of course. Again, please excuse me, señorita. I apologize humbly for the interruption. It was only that Señor Weller insisted I contact you here right away. He made no mention of a vacation. I am sorry to have bothered you."

"It's all right, really, Señor DeBraggo," Suzanne said, shooting a glare of reproof at Hart. "I often mix business with pleasure. It's no problem at all."

DeBraggo smiled. "Then I will await your call, Señorita Cassidy. I am also staying here in the hotel and have written my room number on the back of my card, in case you have the time to look at my jewelry. Until we talk again, at your convenience, of course." He snapped his heels together, then turned and walked away without even so much as a "drop dead and goodbye" to Hart.

He watched the man walk back to his own table. There was something about him that made Hart uneasy. Instinct warned him that the man was not what he seemed, that he was someone who could be very dangerous. Maybe even deadly. The glint in his eyes was too cold and hard.

Hart looked back at Suzanne. "Do you get that sort of thing a lot when you're out?" he asked sharply, unable to rationalize just why his temper was still smoldering. What in hell did he care if the man had insultingly ignored him? Or that Suzanne didn't mind mixing business with pleasure? If indeed that was what had happened. And if it was and his instincts were on the wrong course, it was certainly none of his concern if her partner sicced inconsiderate clients on her.

"No, not often," Suzanne said, staring at De-Braggo's card.

Hart took a long swallow of ice water, hoping the coldness of it would somehow miraculously put a chill on both his overactive libido and his temper. Could he mix business with pleasure? he wondered, watching her. Could he draw her into his arms, kiss her, taste her passion as he'd wanted to for so long and still seriously consider that she could be out to destroy him? That she could be guilty of treason, possibly even murder?

A frown dug deeply into Suzanne's brow as Hart studied her. He suddenly found himself wondering if she could read his thoughts.

"Hart," she said softly, cutting into his musings. He saw new fear in her eyes.

"I didn't tell Clyde what hotel I was going to be staying in."

Hart instantly shoved out of his seat and darted across the restaurant in the direction Salvatore DeBraggo had gone. His gaze swept over the other patrons, but there was no sign of the Spaniard anywhere.

Hart lay on his bed and stared into the darkness, running everything that had happened that evening through his mind again. Right after leaving Suzanne he'd called Private Roubechard about the background checks he'd requested, but there was some problem with getting the files downloaded and transferred from the Armed Security Agency, so they weren't going to be available until morning.

He mulled over the incident at dinner again. Had the whole thing with DeBraggo been a setup? Something the man and Suzanne had staged just for him? Maybe so she could gain a little more of Hart's trust? Look a bit more innocent, a bit more vulnerable, so that he'd believe and help her?

He threw back the sheet and swung his feet to the floor, annoyed by his inability to turn off his thoughts and go to sleep. That wasn't usually a problem. He'd slept in everything from a sagging feather bed to a foxhole to a leaf-filled muddy crevice in the Peruvian jungle. He'd slept through artillery fire, bombing raids and silence so deep it was deafening.

He glanced at the clock on his nightstand. Almost 3:00 a.m. If he wasn't going to sleep, the least he could do was think. Rationally.

Why had she really come back?

Frustrated and annoyed by the traitorous bent of his thoughts, Hart settled down at the desk in his bedroom and flipped on the computer. If his libido and sudden bent for nostalgia kept getting in the way, he was most certainly going to end up either behind bars or dead. Especially if the woman heating his libido and stirring that nostalgia had come to him with a lie and treachery in mind.

He typed a series of codes into his laptop and tried

accessing ASA, but whatever was wrong on their end was still wrong.

Maybe he could do a search for DeBraggo and Suzanne on the Web. He zipped through several search engines before deciding which one to use.

Within five minutes he had pulled up several sites that had something to do with the name DeBraggo. One advertised financial assistance, another was a travel agency in Texas, another a tax attorney in New Mexico and yet another an import/export-business Web site.

None seemed suspicious, but he knew that guilt sometimes had a way of hiding behind a facade of angelic innocence.

He opened the first one, and his brows rose in interest. Their headquarters were based in Los Angeles, California.

A little much for coincidence.

The sound of screeching tires, followed by a crash, suddenly shattered the stillness of the night and Hart's concentration. He ran to the window of his apartment. Two cars were at the corner, the front end of a sporty red foreign job embedded in the passenger door of a sleek black Lincoln twice its size. A cloud of steam rose from the sports car's crushed hood as the two drivers started throwing their arms and hands about, obviously arguing.

Hart stared down at the wreck glistening in the glow of the moon. The steaming sports car reminded him of dancing waves of fire.

Rick's chopper had burst into flames.

Memories assaulted Hart and before he could stop it, time spun backward...

The team had split into pairs, partnering off to

circle their enemy, surround them and move in stealthily for the attack. Rick and Hart had been approaching from the rear, flying low over the Raumsean Woods, several miles inside of Iran's border.

The experimental weapons-detection systems installed in their Cobras warned them of an antiaircraft missile installation hidden within the dense growth of trees below. With that warning they both should have been able to easily avoid any attack and take out their would-be assailant before he even knew they were there.

"Tracker, we got one below," Hart radioed. "You see it?"

"Got it in my sights, Ice," Rick answered, using the name the close-knit group of men in the corps had given Hart not only because of his coolness under pressure, but because each of them, in one way or another, had discovered that he kept his innermost emotions on ice; out of reach or touch.

Hart watched him descend toward his target.

Suddenly a missile shot from the trees.

"Tracker, evade!" Hart ordered. "Evade!"

Rick's Cobra exploded in a burst of flames.

Stunned, unable to believe what he'd just seen, Hart froze. For the briefest of moments he stopped living, as he watched what was left of the burning chopper spiral from the sky, crash into the dense woods and explode again.

Another missile burst from the foliage below.

The instinct for survival rushed in on Hart, and he jerked back on the throttle...

Hart was pulled back to the present by the sound of a police siren. He realized that his only hope of finding out who was trying to destroy him was to turn the tables on them—just as he'd done during that mission. For the briefest of moments that day a year ago he'd stopped being the hunter and had become the prey—a move that had nearly gotten him killed.

It wasn't going to happen again.

He shrugged aside the past and forced himself to concentrate on the here and now, on what he knew about Suzanne Cassidy.

It wasn't much.

He snatched the telephone receiver from the hook. The night before Rick's last mission, she had done the one thing that no pilot could ever forgive. If she was innocent she would have known better.

The thought had nagged at him for the past year. Rick would have trusted her, might even have confided in her—told her things about the corps, about their missions, that he shouldn't have. Things that she might have, in the end, used against him.

Hart punched out the number for her hotel, but the moment the operator came on the line, he hung up. No. Not this way. He needed to look into her eyes when he asked her that question.

A week ago he would have labeled the mere idea of her stealing secret military plans and setting Rick up to be killed ridiculous, the suspicion ugly and totally unwarranted. Now he couldn't discount it, because now he knew all too well that she could have come back to do the same thing to him.

Or was she merely someone's pawn? A total innocent who was being used?

His mind was a jumbled maze of unanswered questions, each filling him with frustration, slicing away at his patience and leaving him too keyed up to even contemplate another attempt at sleep.

He dressed and left the apartment, carrying a brown paper bag in which he'd placed the water glass Suzanne had used at dinner and which he'd managed to slip out of the dining room under his jacket without anyone noticing.

The lab guys at the base weren't going to like being woken up in the middle of the night, but he didn't care. If he was going to find out the truth, this was as good a time as any, and he couldn't think of a better place to start than running her prints and finding out who or what Suzanne Cassidy really was.

All he knew about her was that she'd been Rick's wife, a schoolteacher and had once said she'd grown up in Virginia. But he had to know what else there was. It might be all innocent; then again, it might not.

It was a fact that the Soviets had always had spies in the United States, families who were devout Russian Communists, but who had lived in the U.S. for years, maybe were even born here. They obtained government jobs and top-secret classifications, became scientists, doctors and teachers, and were usually not caught until they'd managed to pass back secrets to the Russians.

And they weren't usually caught until it was too late.

On impulse he stopped by Suzanne's hotel on the way to the base. If she wasn't in her room, he'd take the opportunity to search it. If she was, he'd apologize for his brusqueness earlier, say it had kept him

awake and, in spite of the late hour, ask her down-
stairs for coffee.

As he entered the lobby he heard the chime of
the elevator to his left and glanced toward it.

Suzanne stepped forward as the wood-paneled
doors silently slid open.

Salvatore DeBraggo was beside her.

Chapter 4

It was almost noon when Suzanne pulled her rental car alongside the building that housed Hart's office. She'd meant to arrive earlier, but after he'd left her last night, she'd known she would have a hard if not impossible time getting to sleep, so she'd run down to the hotel lobby to get a book from the gift shop.

The sight of Salvatore DeBraggo standing in the small shop, flipping idly through a magazine, had rattled her, and she'd been about to turn and hurry away when he'd looked up, spotted her and spoken.

"Mrs. Cassidy." His thick accent turned her name to a series of deep, musical rolls.

"Mr. DeBraggo, hello." She felt a tiny bit of relief to realize there were several other people in the gift store. She wasn't alone with him.

"Please, let me apologize again for interrupting your dinner earlier," he said, smiling.

Anger and a bit of bravado melded with her fear,

and she instantly decided to confront his lie. She'd never been one to skirt an issue. "I didn't tell my associate in L.A. where I'd be staying, Mr. De-Braggo."

He nodded. "Ah, my late wife used to tell me I wasn't very good at white lies." He smiled. "I should stop trying."

Suzanne didn't return the smile.

"Yes, well, the truth is, I recognized you from your picture in the *New York Times*—the article they did on your gallery when you purchased the Mastroniani painting from the Brenroget estate last month. I'm afraid when I saw you in the hotel restaurant, impulse overrode my normally good manners." He shrugged. "Again, I apologize."

It had been a coincidence, and Suzanne had chided herself for the dark suspicions she'd harbored about him. Assassin, FBI agent, foreign spy, even privateer and terrorist.

She turned the car ignition off and grabbed her bag. Before leaving for Hart's office she'd made several long-distance calls in regard to the jewelry Mr. DeBraggo wanted to sell. She wasn't certain but something still didn't ring true about him. And she could swear she'd seen one of the pieces before—in a museum.

She'd also placed a call to Clyde, who had suggested she move into a place owned by a friend of his. He'd also badgered her mercilessly for almost fifteen minutes for details about whom she'd gone to dinner with.

The fact that Hart could still stir feelings in her she didn't want stirred had taken her aback yesterday, but she had gathered her wits about her now.

It was merely a physical attraction. That was all it had ever been, and she could handle that.

She stepped from her car and entered the building. She made her way to his office and found his aide standing at the file cabinet just outside. Hart's office door was closed, but she knew he was in there. She'd seen him through the window when she'd climbed out of her car.

She had to be careful.

The aide turned from the cabinet, and Suzanne asked to see Hart.

Even though Hart could hear her voice through his closed door, he'd known the moment she stepped into his aide's office, had been acutely aware of her presence since he'd seen her car pull up outside. Anger and yearning churned within him. He had half hoped that she had left Three Hills and was out of his life forever, and he had feared that was exactly what she would do and he would never seen her again. His feelings didn't make sense, but he was too smart to examine them.

Doubting oneself, examining feelings and trusting women were the three things that turned a man into a fool.

He looked down at the lab report on the drinking glass he'd taken from the hotel dining room. They'd come up with nothing out of the ordinary. According to the fingerprints from DMV and when she'd worked as a clerk in the army before her marriage, Suzanne Cassidy was Suzanne Cassidy. Maiden name Ramsey, middle name Julynne. Her parents had divorced by the time she was eight, father ex-military, mother an artist who'd been married six times.

The preliminary background check Hart's aide had handed him earlier on Suzanne hadn't told him anything different. It was far from complete, and he didn't need to read through it again to know what it said. He'd already gone over it a half-dozen times.

According to it, Suzanne was clean. But Teresa Calderone's record had been clean, too, or so said the feds, and believing that, and them, had nearly gotten Hart and several other members of the Cobra Corps killed.

A little over two years or so ago, the daughter of Peru's staunchest antidrug advocate had been abducted by a member of the drug cartel, and the CIA spooks pulling duty there had requested the corps's help in getting her back. It had been a simple plan: go in, grab her, get out.

The CIA's main contact for information in Peru had been Teresa. Unfortunately, the spooks' background check on her failed to discern that her fiancé had been murdered by a member of the cartel.

Teresa hadn't really cared about rescuing the hostage or aiding the war on drugs. She hadn't even cared about living. All she'd cared about was getting revenge—killing the man who'd ordered the death of her fiancé—and helping the CIA and the Cobra Corps put her in a position to do just that.

But Teresa hadn't done nearly as good a job of seducing the cartel's leader, Guilermo Ortega, as she'd thought, and when she tried to kill him, he'd been ready for her. It was only by sheer luck that Hart had been nearby and heard the struggle. A well-placed fist to the jaw had rendered the older man unconscious, and Hart had gotten Teresa away.

But within seconds Hart and his crew had gone

from being the hunters to the hunted, and after grabbing the young woman, they'd barely escaped Ortega's camp with their lives.

That much could not be said for Teresa Calderone, however. She had broken away from Hart at the last moment and gone back in after Ortega.

As far as Hart knew, no one had ever seen her alive again.

Trusting Teresa Calderone and the CIA's work had been a mistake. The type of mistake he'd vowed he would never let happen again.

"Captain Branson?"

Jerked from his memories, Hart stared at the intercom, experiencing a moment of disorientation as his aide's voice drew him back to the present.

"Ms. Cassidy is here to see you, sir."

Hart looked down at the report that lay open on his desk. Everything in it indicated Suzanne Cassidy was the epitome of the all-American girl. Yet the feds suspected her of treason.

And he suspected her of worse.

He flipped the folder closed, closing off his emotions as well, he opened his office door.

Suzanne was standing beside Roubechard's desk, deep in conversation with the young man. She turned, as if feeling Hart's gaze on her. A white halter top and slacks elegantly draped the subtle curves of her body, accentuated the richness of her dark hair and the creaminess of her skin.

In spite of himself, Hart's eyes drank in the sight of her, and he found it an effort to swallow past the knot that suddenly formed in his chest. She looked beautiful, almost mesmerizing. He damned himself for noticing and his body for reacting.

If he didn't start thinking with his head, instead of another body part, he was doomed.

Maybe she'd been able to sleep because she had nothing to fear. There was no reason for her to toss and turn, to lie awake thinking and worrying because her plans were already in place. It was an ugly suspicion, but one he found all too plausible.

"Good morning, Suzanne," he said calmly, none of the turmoil churning inside of him evident in his tone. He smiled and cloaked himself within the soul-numbing coldness of battle. "Come in."

"Thank you." She brushed past him, her gaze avoiding his.

He watched her move away from him, unable to keep from appreciating the sight. "Would you like a cup of coffee?"

"No, thank you," Suzanne said. She looked around nervously. "Did you get the report on Rick?" Her tone was a little cooler, a little abrupt.

She glanced back at him, and their eyes met for a brief second before she tore her gaze away.

Hart closed the door and returned to his desk as she sat in a chair opposite it.

"Good morning, Suzanne," he said again pointedly, his gaze riveted on her. He knew what she was trying to do. But whereas she intended to try to ignore the physical attraction that obviously still burned between them, Hart had made exactly the opposite decision. He had every intention of using it in whatever way necessary to get to the truth.

Suzanne's smile looked forced. She wound her hands together in her lap, while looking everywhere in his office but at him. "Sorry," she said. "Good morning, Hart. Did you get the report on Rick? Is there anything of significance in it?'' She spoke hurriedly. ''I mean, anything that seems unusual?''

He looked down at the folder containing the report on Rick. There had been nothing in the preliminary background check to indicate that Richard Jonathan Cassidy had been anything other than an honorable and dedicated military officer. Which was what Hart had expected.

''Yes, I got it,'' he said, ''and no, Suzanne, there is nothing out of the ordinary in it.'' But she probably already knew that. He caught her gaze, stared deep into her eyes, searching for reaction, for lies or truth, and felt himself becoming lost.

He pulled himself up, reining in the unwanted feelings. ''Nothing to indicate why the feds would suspect him, *or his wife*,'' he added pointedly, ''of treason.'' He rose and walked to a table by the window, where a coffeepot sat on a warmer, and grabbed one of the cups beside it. ''Sure you wouldn't like a cup of coffee?''

''Yes, I'm sure, but thank you.''

Hart poured himself some coffee and took a long swallow. Hot enough to jar his physical senses, strong enough to jolt his other senses into permanent alert.

What had Rick told her before that mission? The answer should have been nothing. The mission had been top secret. But what if Rick *had* told her something? Possibly just enough to get himself killed?

The findings on Rick's chopper about just why he hadn't been able to maneuver away from the missile had proved inconclusive. Not enough wreckage left and retrieved, Hart remembered the report had said. Best speculation: compressor-blade failure.

Hart moved past Suzanne to resume his seat behind the desk, and a whisper of her perfume drifted to him, a heady scent that teased his senses as much as her beauty, her nearness, teased his desire.

"Whoever is behind all this has to be connected to the Cobra Corps," Suzanne said. "It has to be someone who had direct access to what you were doing on that mission."

Hart's mind cleared and his gaze fell again on Rick's folder, the sight of it and her accusation helping to chase away the subversive thoughts that kept invading his mind.

"Don't you agree?" Suzanne asked when he didn't respond.

He looked at her, stealing her gaze, holding it prisoner—silently interrogating her. "Maybe," he said finally. But even as he voiced agreement, he silently rejected the possibility. The corps was his family. The thought that one of its members could be a traitor, a murderer, was—

He cut off the thought, not even wanting to consider it. Suzanne was a military brat, or at least had been until her parents divorced when she was eight, which meant she knew a lot about military life and procedures. She was the perfect person to pull off this sort of scheme.

Suzanne felt her breath nearly desert her as his gaze held hers pinioned, but instead of nerves or fear, a sense of longing seized her. Flushed, she finally managed to turn away from him. Pushing out of her seat, she walked to the window and stood with her back to him. But she could feel his gaze on her, watching, waiting, assessing her.

Stop it! she ordered herself. If she didn't get hold

of herself, and fast, this was never going to work. She inhaled deeply, memories flashing into her mind.

When she'd realized there was an attraction between them two years ago, she'd been almost thankful. It had been so long since Rick had looked at her with desire in his eyes that she'd begun to feel totally undesirable and to believe that no man would ever look at her that way again.

Then she'd started to look at Hart the way she'd wished Rick would look at her, and the possibilities of what could happen between them had frightened her almost beyond reason. The thought of those possibilities had also brought guilt, which had eaten away at her night and day, even though she'd known the attraction between them was only physical. That was all it had been, all it would ever be.

"I guess I didn't tell you yesterday," he said, "but it is good to see you again, Suzanne."

She turned and smiled. "It's good to see you again, too, Hart. Even under these circumstances." Suzanne felt the beat of her heart accelerate. A rush of heat swept through her that left her trembling.

Part of her felt so right being with him again, and at the same time it felt almost as if Rick's ghost was standing between them, watching and condemning. She sighed. "I wish the circumstances were different, though," she said quietly.

Hart nodded, watching as the sunlight streaming through the office window touched her long hair, turned it to gleaming threads of dark silk and made him want, more than ever, to close the distance between them and run his fingers through her hair and... "Me, too," he said finally, his voice rough with unwanted emotion. "But if this hadn't happened, Suzanne, do you think you would ever have come back here?"

The question was out of his mouth before he'd even been aware he was thinking it. Dammit. It wasn't like he really wanted to know, or even cared.

Suzanne stared, surprised by the question. Did he honestly care? Or was the inquiry meant to lead her into a trap? *Would* she ever have come back, ever found the courage to face him again if she wasn't desperate for his help? She didn't know, so she ignored the question and reached across his desk for the folder that lay there. "Is this the background check you said you were going to have done on Rick?"

Hart grasped her hand before she could pull it and the file away.

Suzanne glanced down at his hand, covering hers. Strong and powerful.

Rick's hands had been like that, too, but she couldn't remember them feeling so warm and tender.

She knew she should pull her hand away. Distance, she told herself. Distance. Just being near him was risky enough. Touching him, letting him touch her, was a danger she didn't need. Yet she remained still, her hand on the file, his hand on hers.

"It's classified," Hart said softly, his gaze holding hers.

"I'm his widow."

Silence and tension screamed through the air as they stared at each other.

"Aren't I?" she finally added, her tone cold, her

own suspicions suddenly exploding. ''Or do you know something I don't?''

Hart released his hold on her hand. She was right. Protocol didn't matter anymore, not if it stood in the way of finding the truth.

She settled back in her chair and read quickly through the report on Rick. A moment later, finished, she looked back at Hart. ''This report isn't very detailed, but you're right, there's nothing unusual in it.'' She lay the folder back on his desk. ''So what do we do next?''

''We start checking out everyone involved in that last mission.''

''What if the person behind this wasn't actually in the corps, Hart? I mean, I know I said he had to be, but what if he's not?'' She looked away, needing to concentrate without having to deal with the emotions that assaulted her every time she looked into Hart's eyes. ''What if he's with the Pentagon or he's some bureaucrat in Washington or something? Then what? We might never find him.''

''No.'' His eyes held hers. ''Whoever stole the plans had to have physical access, and that puts him in the corps, or at least connected to someone in the corps. There were only a certain number of plans, and except for the ones kept under tight security at the base, they were all with the corps on that mission. Every pilot who flew that night had access to the hardware, but only a few had access to the plans, including Rick.''

And you, Suzanne thought.

''If it goes beyond that—'' Hart shrugged ''—we'll just have to see.''

''What do you want me to do?''

"Before you got here I asked my aide to get preliminary background checks on all the corps members who were involved in that mission in any way—pilots, mechanics, strategists, clerks, fuelers, everyone. The reports won't be extremely detailed, but they'll do for a start. If we think we need more, we'll get it, but that'll take longer." He switched on his intercom. "Roubechard, have the other reports arrived yet?"

"Just now, sir," his aide answered. "I'll bring them right in."

Suzanne turned as the door opened and Private Roubechard entered carrying a stack of folders. She watched him cross the room. He was medium height and compactly built, his brown hair extremely close-cropped. He had a face that reminded her of a hawk, eyes that seemed to miss nothing and a tattoo on the back of his left hand that reminded her of a family crest—a shield bearing a horse's head.

Except for the military bearing, haircut and manners, Private Roubechard reminded her of more than a few gang members she'd seen in L.A. He set a box filled with folders on Hart's desk and left the room.

"I don't remember him," Suzanne said.

Hart glanced up from the folders he'd started sorting through. "Marcus Roubechard?" He glanced toward the closed door. "He's only been here a few months."

"Which means he's not a suspect," Suzanne said.

Hart separated the stack of folders. "Roubechard is barely nineteen," he said. "His grandfather was killed in Vietnam, his father in Beirut. The tattoo on his hand is First Cavalry Division. They were both in it. So, no, Suzanne, he's not a suspect.''

She felt like a heel.

Hart handed half the folders to Suzanne. "I'll check the members of the corps," he said. "You start with their family members."

"Family members?" Suzanne looked from the folders to Hart, confused. "Why?"

"You were Rick's wife," Hart said, "and the feds suspect you."

She nodded. "You're right."

Hart sat back in his chair and rubbed his eyes with thumb and forefinger. He was getting nowhere, except frustrated, and he needed a break. "I think I've about had it with this for now. How about we break for a while and drive into town for some lunch?" he suggested.

Suzanne looked up from the file she'd been reading. They hadn't spoken in more than an hour, both intent on getting as much done as possible. "Sure." Her throat was dry, her voice cracking. "Just let me finish this file."

The intercom buzzed. "General Walthorp on the line, sir," Roubechard said.

Hart pushed the responding button and stood. "Hold him a minute." He looked at Suzanne. "My unit is involved in an upcoming training exercise with Walthorp's," he said when she looked up. "He most likely has some questions. I'll take the call out there," he indicated the outer office, "and be right back."

Suzanne nodded, wondering if he was telling her the truth. Perhaps "General Walthorp" was a code name for an FBI agent. Or the man had information about Rick or someone else involved in that mission.

Or maybe he was Hart's accomplice.

The minute Hart stepped from the room Suzanne slapped the file she'd been reading closed and reached for her oversize handbag.

Her mother always said that only a fool ignored opportunity when it knocked.

Suzanne was no fool, and opportunity was definitely knocking now.

She glanced quickly at the door, then turned back to Hart's desk and reached for the stack of files he'd been reading. There had been several men in the Cobra Corps whom Rick had been closer to than any of the others: Hart; Lane Banner, another pilot; Brenner Trent, the corps's chief mechanic; and two rookie pilots—Rand Towler and Zack Morrow.

She'd met them all at one time or another, though she'd only met the two rookie pilots once, about a month before Rick's death.

What she was about to do was likely foolish, not to mention illegal, and Hart might discover her deception immediately and refuse to help her further. But it was a chance she had to take. As she pulled each file from the stack, she slid it quickly into her bag. She stopped when she started to draw out Zack's, and the one underneath it caught her eye. She turned it so she could get a better look at the label attached to its tab. Hart Branson.

Opportunity's knock became a thunderous thud.

She shoved the folder on Hart into her bag with the others. There might be nothing in any of the files—but she wanted to look them over personally later, not merely take Hart's word for what was in them. Especially whatever was in his.

She rearranged the remaining file folders on his desk, thankful there were several dozen; the absence of the few she'd taken wouldn't be readily noticeable. He reentered just as she finished.

"Ready for lunch now?" he asked.

Suzanne stood. "I'm sorry, Hart, I forgot that I promised to meet Mr. DeBraggo this afternoon to give him an appraisal on the jewelry he wants to sell. Remember, the man from the restaurant?"

It was a lie—she'd arranged only to call De-Braggo—but the need to see the files and put some distance between Hart and herself was almost overwhelming.

Hart nodded. He thought about following her now, but the general wanted to meet with him in an hour, and there was no way he could follow her and count on being back in time for the meeting. And Walthorp was one old codger he knew better than to stand up. He dropped the file folders back into the box Roubechard had delivered them in. "Dinner, then," Hart said.

The phone on his desk rang. He picked up the receiver and motioned for Suzanne to wait a minute, intending to quickly dismiss whoever was calling. But it turned out to be a call he couldn't make short.

Suzanne started for the door.

Hart covered the mouthpiece with his hand. "Seven," he said softly, as the man on the other end of the line began to talk about a situation heating up in Mexico and the possibility of sending in the Cobra Corps.

She closed the door softly behind her.

What if Suzanne was telling the truth? Hart suddenly wondered. What if her life really was in jeopardy, and he went on a mission and left her alone?

Suzanne tossed her bag into the car.

"Suzanne?"

She turned to see Chief Carger walking toward her. "Chief," she said, inwardly cringing, outwardly smiling.

He lit a cigarette. "You planning on joining the army now?"

She laughed, fully aware that the comment was intended to secure him the reason she was back in Three Hills. But that was something she couldn't divulge. "Hardly, Chief," she said. "I'm an antiques dealer now. I have a gallery in Los Angeles." She remembered Salvatore DeBraggo. "I was just in the area on business for a client, so I thought I'd drop in and see Captain Branson."

The chief nodded, exhaling a cloud of smoke. "Well, glad to hear everything's okay and all. I mean, that you're just visiting. The captain's a nice enough guy, but I never got the impression he was the marrying kind." He offered a warm smile. "If you know what I mean."

She didn't, but she wasn't going to ask. Evidently the chief didn't like Hart. But there could be a million reasons, she told herself. And most likely all of them had to do with the army, not her.

Or did the chief know something about Rick's death? Something that linked Hart to it as more than a mere witness? Had his comment been meant as a warning?

Chapter 5

Six-thirty. He'd arrived purposely early. Hart glanced at the slip of paper he'd tossed onto the passenger seat. Before Suzanne left his office earlier, she'd written down directions to the bungalow she'd rented and given them to Roubechard to give to him.

Obviously she planned on staying around awhile.

Hart glanced at his watch again. If Suzanne was like most women he'd dated, she wouldn't be ready, and that might give him time to look around the place without her realizing it.

He stood beside the car and looked at the small ranch-style adobe. Pale brown paint, turquoise trim, tile roof. Standard Southwestern style. Rocks and a variety of small cacti framed the pathway to the front door.

He pushed the doorbell and heard a series of chimes ring inside.

Several seconds passed.

She didn't answer.

Hart glanced at the rental car sitting in the driveway, then toward a slightly open window next to the door. Soft music drifted out past the lace curtains. He looked through the window and found he could see straight to the rear of the house. A sliding glass door was open to the patio. She was sitting on a chaise longue.

He followed the brick path that led around the small house, but as he approached the rear he heard Suzanne's voice and stopped.

"Yes, I know it's late," she said.

Hart peeked around the corner and saw that she was on a cell phone.

"But the package should go out in a day or two. No more." She paused. "Yes, it will go out once we confirm the payment has been made," she said, and rose, but remained standing beside the chair.

Hart stepped behind the tall rosebush that grew at the corner of the house and watched her through the gnarled branches of the plant.

Suzanne nodded, as if her caller could see her, then walked to the far edge of the patio and stared at the endless expanse of desert.

She was wearing a long, white terry-cloth robe, dark glasses, and her hair was covered by some kind of cloth turban.

"Direct deposit will be fine," she said a moment later. "Yes, within two days, if nothing goes wrong."

Every suspicion and doubt he'd had about her suddenly threatened to overwhelm him. Anger turned his blood to fire, while resentment chilled it. He knew her words could be perfectly innocent, but giving anyone the benefit of the doubt, especially when his career, maybe even his life, was at stake, wasn't something he was about to do. Not even for Suzanne.

She gazed out at the horizon after terminating the call as if deep in thought, then she finally turned, set the phone down on a nearby table and walked into the house.

Hart waited what seemed like several excruciatingly long minutes, but she didn't return for the cell phone. He moved stealthily across the patio, grabbed the phone and stepped back out of sight of the glass door.

Without giving himself time to rethink his intentions, he pushed the redial button. A series of clicks sounded, then the line began to ring on the other end.

''*Oui,* Marsei residence.''

Hart cursed and instantly broke the connection.

Only an hour ago he'd learned that the man the feds suspected of buying the stolen plans was a renowned French spy who worked freelance for any government, terrorist group, revolutionary or crackpot who could pay his price. His name was Robert Marsei.

Coincidence? Hart's hand tightened around the small cell phone as the insane urge to throw it as far as he could into the desert almost overwhelmed him. But that wouldn't solve anything, and even though Marsei was not an uncommon French name, Hart didn't believe in coincidence.

He drew in a deep breath in an effort to calm himself, placed the phone back on the patio chair and hurried around to the front of the bungalow.

Hopefully she hadn't looked out the front window and seen his car parked at the curb. She'd wonder where he was.

Then again, maybe she knew. Maybe she'd seen him drive up, knew he'd overheard her and left the phone out there on purpose, suspecting he'd do exactly what he had done.

But why would she do that?

He didn't have an answer. He only knew it was a possibility.

He knocked on the door again, and she opened it almost immediately.

Suzanne felt her pulse instantly accelerate and her heart begin to beat just a little faster as her eyes met his. It had been only mere hours since she'd seen him last, but her gaze involuntarily raked over him as if it had been years. He hadn't worn his uniform. Instead, dark-brown slacks covered his long, lean legs and made them seem even longer, a white dress shirt tried, but failed, to completely obscure a wall of muscular chest, and a brown leather jacket accentuated his broad shoulders.

"Come in," she finally managed, surprised by the breathlessness she heard in her voice.

He stepped past her and into the living room, his gaze quickly taking in the furnishings. "Nice place, but why'd you leave the hotel?" He turned back to watch her as she closed the door, then stood facing him but not approaching.

"Oh, I really dislike hotels and—" she shrugged "—I was talking to Clyde this morning and he suggested if I was going to be here a few days, that I move into this place. It belongs to a friend of his who spends most of his time in L.A."

Hart nodded. "Makes sense." He glanced around again. Whoever it was who owned the bungalow definitely wasn't hurting for money. Everything in it appeared expensive.

"I just have to grab a wrap and my bag, and I'll be ready to go."

He wanted her, and silently cursed. He'd been trying to keep his mind occupied with suspicions and anything else he could fill it with, but the thought pounded repeatedly through Hart's head now as his gaze devoured the sight of her and his body began an instant simmer.

The robe, glasses and turban were gone. Now long waves of dark hair cascaded over her bare shoulders, while a simple, dark-rust silk sheath slid provocatively over every curve and line of her body, complementing and accentuating the copper-hued slivers of color in her brown eyes.

Desire, hot and hungry, coiled inside him like a rope of fire. No other woman had ever affected him so thoroughly and swiftly, but if he had learned nothing else in his life, he'd learned caution and self-control.

And as he reminded himself of all his suspicions, a cold wave of anger and sense of survival doused his desire. Yet life's hard experiences and his intense army training allowed him to keep the fire of seduction in his eyes and a smile on his lips.

Hart wasn't able to get the idea that they'd been followed out of his mind. He looked around the restaurant again. He'd noticed a dark car parked down the street from her house as they'd left. It had pulled out right after them and stayed on their tail, though a respectable distance away, for some time as they'd driven to the restaurant.

Several blocks before they'd arrived at the restaurant, it had turned off, but he still suspected whoever had been driving, most likely a fed, had been following them.

The Italian restaurant was elegant, with a rustic touch. And it was quiet.

It reminded Suzanne of a quaint café in northern Italy that she'd once visited as a teenager while on a trip with her mother and one of her stepfathers. She didn't remember which one. Except for her own father, whom she'd seen only a handful of times a year after her parents divorced, the rest of the men in her mother's life were little more than a blur.

Suzanne set down her wineglass and glanced at what was left of her fettuccine and chicken. It was her favorite dinner, but she'd barely eaten any of it.

But it wasn't the thought of rotting away in some federal prison that had been lurking in the back of her mind for days that had stolen her appetite. It was being with Hart again. Nerves. She stole a glance at him, and a rush of feeling swept through her that she didn't want to acknowledge or try to understand.

"It must have been hard for you," Hart said, breaking the silence between them, "starting over."

She looked back at him, wondering if she should read anything into his words other than what she'd heard. Shrugging, she said casually, "It was and it wasn't," not willing to go into detail.

She'd decided long ago that she would never be like her mother. Lyla Russell seemed to have spent her entire life falling in and out of love and was now on her sixth—or was it her seventh?—husband. Suzanne had lost count.

But even if Rick had come back safely from that last mission, she would have had to start her life over. Their life together had ended the night before he left. That, however, was something she had never admitted to anyone.

"Do you still miss him?"

The question jarred Suzanne from her musings and echoed through her mind. *Did she miss him?* She thought for a moment. She missed the man she *thought* she'd married, but not the one it turned out she *had* married. "Yes," she said, knowing it was the answer Hart expected. "I do."

Jealousy flared in Hart, hot and unanticipated, sweeping through him, startling him, before he could even attempt to deny or ignore it. He didn't know why he still wanted her after all this time, after everything that had happened. What the hell was the matter with him? It hadn't been that long since he'd been with a woman. "Yeah, I do, too," he managed. He looked deep into her eyes, and again suspicion overruled the feelings he hadn't welcomed.

The look he saw there didn't agree with her words.

Suzanne played a fingertip around the rim of her wineglass, her thoughts on both men. Rick had stood barely five-nine; Hart was several inches over six feet. Rick's build had been muscular compaction, his facial features a carving of perfection, his handsomeness a classical one, and combined with his limitless charm, no one, male or female, had been able to resist him.

Hart's physique was long and lean, and his face

was coarsely featured, like a sculptor's work in progress. "Granite" was the term that came to mind as she looked at the nose whose slight bump on the ridge hinted at a long-ago break; at the unyielding jawline; at the high cheekbones that reminded her of desert ridges. But looking into his eyes was like becoming lost in a midnight sky strewn with stars.

How many times in the past had she stolen endless moments staring at those eyes when he was occupied with something else, knowing that if she let herself look too long she might find it was a place she'd never want to leave? How many times had she dreamed of running her fingers through his hair or wondered how his lips would feel against hers?

And his voice. God, how she'd missed hearing that deep, soothing drawl that was part Louisiana and part Texas.

There seemed both intense strength and a quiet vulnerability about Hart. It was a combination she'd always found odd—and all too appealing.

"So," Hart said, drawing her from what he assumed were thoughts of the past, and himself from a quandary of emotion he'd rather ignore. "Other than moving to Los Angeles, making new friends and starting a new career, what else have you been doing? Are you seeing anyone? Involved? Engaged?"

He saw the small smile that tugged at the corners of her mouth. Jealousy reared in him again, but he told himself he really didn't care if she was romantically involved with someone, unless that person was also her accomplice in treason and setting him up for a fall. He was just making conversation, try-

ing to find out as much about her as possible in order
to get a direction toward the truth.

Hart knew his question had brought thoughts of
a man into her mind, as he'd intended it to. What
he wanted to know was who.

"Too personal?" he asked when she didn't answer.

Suzanne looked back at him. Innocence shone in
her eyes, but it had shone in Teresa Calderone's
eyes, too, and he had no intention of falling into a
trap like that again.

The report that had come back that morning on
Suzanne had been clean. But that didn't mean there
weren't things about her that hadn't been discerned
yet. After all, it had merely been a preliminary report and one done in a hurry.

If she was guilty, and he had to consider that a
very real possibility, it was only logical she had an
accomplice. Hell, she could have a whole country
behind her for all he knew.

"No," Suzanne said finally, jerking Hart from his
speculations. "There's no man in my life. Unless
you count my cat, Dooby, or my business partner,
Clyde, who is also my cousin, and more in love with
antiques than I think he could ever be with a
woman."

"The man obviously doesn't know what he's
missing," Hart said.

Or maybe he does, a nasty little voice in the back
of his mind whispered, reminding him of the treachery and betrayal he'd been handed from women he'd
thought had loved him.

"What about you?" Suzanne asked, a teasing lilt

to her tone. "Why hasn't some lucky woman caught you yet?"

A sense of longing sliced through Hart, totally unexpected and almost painful.

She's responsible for Rick's death, he reminded himself, trying to ward off the feelings he didn't want to have. And the feds suspect her of treason.

But they also think Rick's alive.

He forced a smile and damned his nagging suspicions while trying to ignore the almost feral need to reach across the table and slip a hand behind her neck, pull her to him and kiss her until he stole the breath from her lungs and the truth from her heart.

"Like you said, Suzanne," he answered finally, "she's been lucky."

She shook her head. "No, I would say she's been very unlucky."

"I'd almost forgotten how wonderful the scent of the desert is," Suzanne said as Hart walked beside her on the path to her bungalow. They hadn't talked about the situation that had brought her back to Three Hills, and she was thankful. For a few hours she had been able to forget the disaster that had taken over her life. She paused at the door and turned to him. "I had a wonderful time tonight, Hart. Thank you."

Obviously she wasn't going to invite him in. Because she needed to report in to her accomplice?

Hart caught her gaze with his, seeking the truth there, and for one brief moment, one millisecond of eternity, he found himself wanting nothing more than to forget his suspicions, forget the world, forget everything, except how much he wanted her.

She was so close.

Now the passion that had always simmered, quietly and denied, between them, suddenly flared into an inferno Hart was helpless to douse. It consumed him, devouring his blood and replacing it with the fires of a need stronger than anything he'd ever felt. It stole his good sense, banished all reason and made a mockery of the self-control that he'd honed to steel-hard perfection over the years, and that he normally could rely on to get him through anything.

His arms swept around her, dragging her into his embrace, crushing her body to him, and his mouth captured hers, swiftly and thoroughly, much like a hunter captures its prey, with little mercy and no tenderness. War and battle, anger and resentment, those were the form of his life and always had been. No one and nothing had ever taught him how to take what he wanted with a gentle hand.

But as much as having her in his arms stoked the conflagration of passion in him, it also stoked the flames of anger. She had been Rick's wife, and she had gotten him killed. The thought echoed cruelly through Hart's mind, slicing at his passion.

He wanted to punish her for Rick, and he wanted to punish her for making him want her. But he couldn't, because she was kissing him back. Her lips sweet, intoxicating and as hungry as his.

A firestorm claimed his body.

Nothing made sense. Reality slipped away. Desire consumed his every thought.

She was everything he'd always wanted and everything he knew he should avoid. She was as much the light he'd always needed in his life as she was the darkness that could destroy him; she was whatever hope he had for the future and a prospect of doom beyond his worst nightmares.

Her arms encircled his neck.

Willpower deserted him. A need fiercer than anything he'd ever experienced consumed him.

It was a kiss of desperation, fueled by such emotional intensity that reality slipped totally away from him. He felt her tongue entwine about his, dueling, teasing and inviting.

A soft moan slipped from her mouth to his, ripping through him, feeding his passion.

Suzanne pressed against Hart, every inch of her body responding to his kiss, his touch. She knew she was losing herself. Hart was the soldier, but she felt the rage of battle erupt deep down within herself. She wanted him, had wanted him for so long…yet every thought and feeling she had was urging her to push him away as much as pull him closer.

He could save her…or he could damn her to a hell beyond imagination.

Suddenly the sound of gunfire erupted behind them, shredding the night's peaceful silence.

Hart ripped away from Suzanne, at the same time grabbing her arms. "Get down," he snarled, and roughly shoved her to the ground, instinctively turning his back to the assault and shielding her with his body.

Another explosion rent the air.

Suddenly he knew it wasn't gunfire. Hart pushed to his feet, his heart hammering against his ribs as much from leftover fear as anger at himself for what he knew had been a senseless mistake. He whirled around to face whoever was out there.

An old car, battered and nearly paintless, coughed and backfired again as it disappeared around the corner.

Hart stared after it, chagrined beyond belief. An ugly curse sped through his mind.

"I thought someone was shooting at us," Suzanne said, breaking the now unearthly stillness that surrounded them.

Hart helped her to her feet, feeling like a fool. He was a soldier. Not once had he ever mistaken any other sound for gunfire. Until now.

"I'll talk to you tomorrow," he said curtly. Without waiting for her to respond, he turned on his heel and stalked to his car.

Mistaking a backfire for gunfire wasn't the only mistake he'd made tonight. He slid into the Vette. What the hell did he think he was doing, kissing her like that? He was falling into an age-old trap, the one every woman used when she wanted something from a man. They were always sweet and cloying when they were trying to gain your trust, then when they had it, they unfailingly betrayed it.

But this was Suzanne, a little voice of reason said from the back of his mind. He scoffed aloud. And the woman who'd left him in a motel room had been his mother.

Desperation allowed him to drudge up memories he normally avoided. If they didn't divert his thoughts and douse the desire smoldering in him, he knew nothing would...

"Stay here, sweetie," Corie Branson had said, "and be a good boy, okay?"

"Can I watch more cartoons, Mommy?" Hart had

said, already turning his attention back to the television.

"Of course, sweetie. Now remember, I love you," she said, pulling the blanket up and tucking it around his legs. "Give Mommy a kiss."

That had been the last time he'd ever seen his mother.

Long hours later he'd awoken when the motel manager, a tall woman, and a policeman entered the room. They'd been nice, and the policeman had given Hart a candy bar while the woman brushed his hair, told him not to be afraid and helped him on with his jacket. Then they'd taken him to a large place where a lot of other children were.

He hadn't understood what was happening then. It was later that they'd explained that his mother had telephoned the police and said she couldn't come back, but that she loved her little boy and asked them to take care of him.

It was a nice lie woven around a shred of truth and meant to keep him from being afraid and crying, and it did—for a while.

But regardless of what the social workers and women at the orphanage said, the one thing Hart had come to realize while growing up was that his mother had left him, with no intention of ever coming back.

His memories rolled on like a kaleidoscope of horror, tearing painfully at his heart, but succeeding in keeping his thoughts of Suzanne from his mind, and desires from conquering his body.

The authorities had taken him to his only relative—an aunt. But she'd already had six children of her own and a worthless husband. The last thing she'd wanted was another child, especially one that wasn't even hers.

His first foster mother had been a nice grandmotherly type who had a sadistic streak a mile wide.

His second loved him like her own, or so he'd thought. After a while he'd finally dropped his defenses and let himself return her love. But it had been a mistake. Two days before the adoption papers were to be signed, she'd backed out. He'd never known why.

Hart spent the remainder of his growing-up years in the orphanage, refusing to care about anyone or expect them to care about him.

Then he'd met Francie, fallen madly in love and gotten married. Six months later he came home one day to find her in bed with one of her brother's friends. A quickie divorce had followed, he'd nearly pickled his brain in booze over the next several months, and finally, in a last-ditch effort to save himself, he'd buried his feelings so deep down he could ignore them—usually—and joined the army.

Hart sighed, realizing that no matter how many unpleasant memories he dredged up, thoughts of Suzanne would still be waiting for him when he was done torturing himself.

Her claim of spies, accidents that weren't accidents and being followed all sounded ludicrous. Now he knew that in spite of all his doubts, suspicions and so-called good sense, part of him obviously wanted to believe her.

Maybe already did.

It was stupid, unprofessional and most likely suicidal. He sighed, but part of him believed her.

A few minutes later Hart swung the Vette onto

the narrow country road that led to the base. He
needed answers, and now was as good a time as any
to try to get them.

Suzanne stood on the porch and watched him
drive away, then remained there long after she'd
seen the taillights disappear around a corner.

Why had she kissed him like that? He didn't trust
her, didn't believe her, was probably playing her
along, hoping she'd confess to treason, murder and
Lord knew what else, and she'd fallen right into his
arms like a fool.

She was just about to go inside when she noticed
another car moving up the street, its headlights out.

Instinctively, she stepped from beneath the porch-
light's glow and into the shadow of a tall saguaro
that grew next to the front door.

Across the street one of her neighbors had a lamp
at the end of his driveway. She watched as the car
pulled past it. A sharp gasp grabbed her lungs. She
wasn't sure, but the man behind the wheel appeared
to be in uniform.

Suddenly all her doubts about Hart disappeared
as if they didn't exist. Alarm seized her.

Once the car passed, she ran into the house, slamming the door behind her. Someone was following
Hart.

She hurled herself into the kitchen and grabbed
the telephone receiver from its wall hook. He had to
be warned. Suzanne stared at the keypad, suddenly
realizing she didn't have his number or know if he
even had a cell phone.

Thoughts of spies and murderers hammered at

her. She ran into the bedroom, grabbed her bag and searched through it for her car keys.

Slamming back out the front door, Suzanne paused, breathless, on the porch.

It was too late. The other car was gone.

The phone was ringing when Hart entered his apartment.

"Hart?" Suzanne said when he picked up.

His heart skipped a beat as alarm seized him. "Suzanne, what's wrong?"

"Nothing. I mean, not with me, but I think someone was following you when you left here. I saw a car pass by a minute or so after you drove away, and it didn't have its lights on, and…"

She leaned against the wall and closed her eyes, realizing she sounded hysterical and he probably didn't believe her.

"I was…worried," she said haltingly, suddenly feeling foolish. She had probably imagined the car had been following Hart. Just like she'd imagined the driver had looked like Chief Carger. Most likely it was just one of her neighbors on his way somewhere. "I was obviously wrong, Hart. You're fine. It's late," she knew she was babbling, but she was unable to stop—because she didn't want to hang up. "I should go. Let you get some sleep. I've probably fantasized this whole mess. Rick always said I had an overactive imagination. I'll talk to you tomorrow."

"Suzanne," Hart said before she could hang up, "I'm fine."

"I know. Really." Her laugh sounded fragile, even to her own ears. "It was probably just one of the neighbors. Hadn't turned his lights on yet, that's all. Good night, Hart.''

Before he could respond again, she hung up.

Hart slowly replaced the receiver while a barrage of conflicting emotions and thoughts assaulted him. Was she right? Had someone followed him when he'd left her place? Or was this another move on her part to catch him off guard to get him to believe her wild claims?

He walked to the window and, careful to move the blinds only fractionally, peered outside.

There was no one in sight and no strange car parked on the street.

But he knew better than to think that meant someone wasn't there.

If the feds suspected he was Suzanne's accomplice in treason and murder, then it made sense they'd have someone tailing him.

He was just about to drop the window blind when he spotted a long, dark car rolling out of sight around the corner, its lights out.

Was that the car Suzanne had seen and thought was following him?

"Ah, hell." He turned away from the window. It was definitely time to call it a night.

Half an hour later his thoughts were still in turmoil. He lay in bed, staring through the darkness at nothing as that moment on her porch played over and over in his mind. He'd drawn Suzanne into his arms, kissed her, crushed her body to his. He'd been out of control, and he'd felt more alive with her body pressed to his than he had in more than a year—maybe in his entire, sorry life.

But was she an innocent being framed or was she

more cunning and deceitful than any woman he'd ever known?

He shifted position, ramming a fist into his pillow out of frustration.

"Dammit." Hart pushed off the bed and began to pace the room. In spite of the confusion and anger simmering in him, he had never wanted a woman as much as he wanted Suzanne Cassidy. But to believe her innocent threatened everything he'd made of his life.

If the government he worked for, the country he had put his life on the line for, was involved in trying to frame an innocent woman, maybe even kill her, and now intended to take him down with her, then his entire life, everything he believed in, was a total sham.

But to believe her guilty meant...

He slammed a fist down on his dresser. No matter which way he looked at the situation, no matter which way it turned out, he was damned.

Chapter 6

Suzanne's tongue slipped between Hart's lips, and a moan of pleasure was torn from his throat.

"Temptress," he growled, the word meant as both homage and curse, the torment of his need turning his voice ragged and harsh.

She clung to him, her arms tightening around his neck, fingers entwining in the golden hair at his nape, as if she never intended to let go.

Fire erupted in his veins, longing tore at his insides, burning deeper, hotter, brighter, than anything he'd ever felt.

His hand moved to cup her breast, and a faint voice at the back of his mind yelled at him to stop—or he would be forever sorry.

Waves of need ripped through his gut as incessant alarms sounded far-off in the back of his mind.

Hart's eyes shot open when the ring of the phone echoed through the room.

He sat up and looked around, momentarily disoriented.

The phone rang again.

He glanced at the empty space of bed beside him. She wasn't there. God, he was totally losing it.

At the phone's next ring he jerked around and grabbed the receiver. ''What?'' he snapped.

''Captain Branson?''

He recognized his aide's voice and instantly sobered. The last time he'd received a call at home in the middle of the night, he had been on his way to Bosnia in less than an hour. ''Yes, Roubechard. What is it?'' Hart glanced at the clock on his nightstand.

Eight a.m.

That wasn't possible. He'd just fallen asleep. He glanced at the watch on his wrist.

''I was boxing up the files you were using yesterday, sir,'' Roubechard said, ''and, uh, I was wondering if you took any of them home with you, sir?''

''No, I told you I was finished with them. Why?''

''Well, uh, Personnel just called and said several files are missing.''

Hart cursed silently. He hadn't taken them, which meant Suzanne had. But why? They'd been going over them in his office together. If she'd wanted to see any of them again, she didn't have to steal them.

''Verify which ones they think are missing,'' Hart said. ''I'll be there shortly.'' He suddenly remembered Suzanne asking about Roubechard.

''No, he is not a suspect.'' His own words taunted him. Could he be wrong? Was it possible Roubechard was involved in this in some way? A fed plant, maybe?

"Yes, sir. But there's more, sir."

Hart felt his insides wince. He didn't need more. "What?"

"I checked on Ms. Cassidy's movements in the last few weeks, sir, like you requested."

He had a feeling that whatever was coming wasn't good.

"She took a trip to France at the end of last month, but once she got off the plane in Paris, sir, she, uh, disappeared."

"What do you mean *she disappeared?*" Hart demanded. It was worse than he'd thought.

"I mean, I couldn't find any trace of where she'd gone, sir. And upon her return to the States," Roubechard went on hurriedly, "she sent a package back to Paris—air express."

A package. Ugly suspicions exploded in his mind. A trip to France...most likely to see Marsei...a package sent there. Had it contained the stolen military plans?

It was all too real a possibility.

Hart knew he should get to the base. There were things he had to do that had nothing at all to do with Suzanne or the investigation into his own background, but which needed to be done.

That was what he should do.

Instead, he stalked up the path to her bungalow and rapped a fist on the front door. If she had taken the files, and he felt there was very little *if* involved, then he wanted her to explain why, and he wanted her to explain right now.

But she didn't answer. He glanced toward the window. When he'd come to the house before, music had been drifting out. Now the curtains were drawn, the house silent and locked. He walked to the side of the house, but her rental car wasn't in the carport.

Was she gone or just out?

He felt the bottom drop out of his gut at the thought that she'd left for good. As soon as the thought and feeling assaulted him, a string of nasty curses zipped through his mind.

Hart stalked back to the Vette and slid behind the wheel. His day had started off lousy, and was continuing its descent with runaway speed.

Two blocks from Suzanne's house a dark car pulled out of a driveway in front of him. He slammed on his brakes and the car sped off. Hart stared after it, certain his eyes were playing tricks. He'd only gotten a glimpse of the driver, but could have sworn it was DeBraggo.

He jammed the Vette into gear and headed for the base. The training exercise he'd scheduled was to begin in an hour. After that he had a meeting with General Walthorp, several reviews to process and a lot of paperwork he didn't even want to contemplate.

The first thing he did when he walked into his office, however, was call Suzanne and leave a message on her machine. "I had a nice time last night, Suzanne, and was hoping we could have dinner again tonight." He strained to keep a hint of seduction in his voice and his anger tightly under control. There had been nothing damning or top secret in any of the files, so why had she taken them? "Maybe at Cactus Jack's." It was one of the most romantic spots in Tucson, and perfect for the type of subtle interrogation Hart had in mind for Suzanne. "I'll pick you up at eight. Call me if that's not okay."

He hung up, then glared at the phone. Maybe confronting her now was a mistake. Instead, maybe he should play along with her game and see where it led.

Hart pulled his car to the side of the road a short distance from Suzanne's bungalow. He'd purposely arrived early again, but this time to watch, not search.

Every house in the neighborhood sat on about an acre of land, most of which remained unlandscaped and wild. Tall saguaro cacti grew profusely in the area, like proud sentries guarding their harsh surroundings, while the smaller fishhook, prickly pear and a dozen other varieties, along with sagebrush and wild grasses, dotted the terrain and turned it to a profusion of color most people didn't expect to see in the desert.

The sun was already well on its way down, so once he cut his lights and engine, the sleek black sports car blended with the dusky night.

Hart sat back in his seat and looked at his surroundings, paying close attention to everything, but most particularly the bungalow. Light flowed from its wide windows, and every once in a while he thought he saw Suzanne walk past one.

He didn't know what he was waiting for, but then, he hadn't known what he was waiting or watching for that night in Peru, either. He'd only known he'd felt an inexplicable and nagging uneasiness. Then

he'd seen Teresa Calderone where she wasn't supposed to be.

And if he hadn't been waiting and watching, he'd
be a dead man.

The lights of a car illuminated the rear of the
Vette.

Hart hunkered down in his seat as it passed, then
felt his pulse race as he watched the car pull to the
curb in front of Suzanne's bungalow.

Salvatore DeBraggo climbed from a glistening,
black luxury sedan.

Hart stiffened. What the hell was DeBraggo doing
here? Picking up stolen plans, maybe?

A moment later Suzanne opened her front door
and the man disappeared inside.

Five minutes passed.

Hart's normally steel-cold nerves gnawed impatiently.

A woman strolled by, walking a dog.

Hart swore softly, a habit that was beginning to
get out of control. Who in blazes was DeBraggo?

He didn't think she'd welcome a federal agent
into her place, at least not knowingly, but the alter-
natives were worse.

Maybe DeBraggo was exactly who and what he'd
claimed to be: a man trying to sell his late wife's
jewelry. But Hart didn't think so.

The door to the bungalow opened, and DeBraggo
stepped out and walked rapidly to his car. He wasn't
carrying anything.

Suzanne remained on the doorstep, watching as
his car moved down the street in the opposite direction from where Hart was parked.

Once it was gone she turned and looked directly at Hart.

He froze. Had she seen him? Did they know he'd been watching them?

Suzanne stepped back into the bungalow and closed the door.

Hart released a hesitant sigh of relief and started his car.

A man jogged past.

Several houses down on the opposite side of the street, another man retrieved a newspaper from the end of his driveway, glanced toward the Vette, then went back into the house.

The neighborhood seemed unusually busy to-night. Or was he merely becoming paranoid? Hart wondered as he pulled up to the bungalow, got out and headed toward the front door.

She opened the door to his knock almost immediately.

"Hart," Suzanne said, smiling.

Welcoming him? Or relieved he hadn't arrived a few minutes earlier?

"I saw Mr. DeBraggo leave," he said, deciding to take a shot at the truth and see where it led.

Suzanne paused, her hand on the clutch bag she'd been about to pick up. She turned. Had he been watching her? "He brought by some of his wife's jewelry." She disappeared into her bedroom and returned carrying a small box. "A beautiful old brooch, a pair of earrings and a gold bracelet." She held the open box toward him. "The brooch is a cameo and, though I'm still new at this, my guess is it's not only genuine, but will bring him a nice price at auction."

Hart looked at the jewelry sitting in the satin-lined box. He didn't know a thing about cameos, earrings or any other kind of jewelry. It could all be fake, a cover meant to convince him DeBraggo was what he claimed and not her partner, if they got caught together, like they just had. "What's a 'nice price'?" he asked, curious.

"Well..." She pulled her gaze from Hart's and looked at the brooch. He was testing her. "Some women would pay a thousand dollars for such a beautiful piece of jewelry, but to a serious cameo collector the price could go into the thousands. Five, ten." She shrugged. "You just never know."

Hart looked from the jewelry to Suzanne, into her eyes. Part of him wanted to believe her, even when he knew he shouldn't.

Cactus Jack's was Southwestern comfort mixed with just the right amount of elegance. Candles on the tables, fine linen and silver, flowers everywhere, a fantastic view of the mountains framing Tucson and food to die for.

But Hart wasn't interested in any of those attributes, unless they aided him in getting what he wanted from Suzanne. And what he wanted was the truth.

"Hart, I'm really worried," Suzanne said after they'd ordered and the waiter had left the table. What she really meant was that she was becoming more frightened, but she didn't want to say that. "Every background check I looked at on every family member of the men in the Cobra Corps appears clean, and I assume, since you haven't said differently, that the ones you checked on the men themselves are clean, too.''

He nodded. She was good.

''So that leads us nowhere, unless you've come up with something else?''

''No.''

She could feel her panic level rising. ''What if we don't find anything?''

He shrugged. ''We go to prison. Or worse.''

Her eyes widened at the answer and the casualness he'd purposely instilled in his tone.

''That's not funny.''

''It wasn't meant to be,'' Hart said. If he had to use fear to get to her, he would.

She took a long swallow of water and set the glass down with a hand that was obviously trembling. ''What do we do next?''

''We keep looking,'' he said softly, hoping the benign answer would reassure her. ''Keep digging.'' Steeling himself against any emotion but the cold, hard anger he'd been honing to perfection all day, he reached across the table and placed his hand over hers.

The preparation hadn't been enough.

Fire assaulted his senses the moment he touched her. Need and want plunged through him, seized him mercilessly and threatened to never let go. Damn. Why did he react to her like that? Especially when he knew that, if nothing else, she was at least a thief?

Suzanne had seen the wariness in his eyes the moment she'd opened the door to him earlier. Something had happened to bring back all his suspicions of her. Yet he was trying to act as if nothing was wrong, and for some reason, that scared her more than anything.

"But what if we don't find anything, Hart?" she persisted. "Regardless of how deep we dig?" The mere touch of his hand on hers stirred feelings she didn't want stirred and instilled a tremor in her voice she couldn't hide. She felt an insane urge to throw herself into his arms and beg him to believe her, to protect her, to—

Stop it! She ordered, suddenly afraid of her own thoughts.

"Let's not talk about spies, lies and dark *what-if*s tonight," Hart said as if reading her mind and sensing her fear.

In spite of the reassuring words and the desire his gesture ignited in her, Suzanne's fears remained.

Hart moved his thumb tenderly, teasingly, over the crest of her knuckles and tried to ignore the passion the gesture threatened to spark within him. He had to play this out and learn what she was up to, how deep her involvement was. "Tell me more about what you've been doing the past year, Suzanne," he said. "What's your new career like? Your new life?"

Her thoughts spun. How much should she tell him? She'd never been very good at lies and pretense. "I live in L.A. now," she started, choosing her words carefully. "I rent a small house in the valley. It was built in the thirties by some movie star." She laughed, but he heard the nervousness in it.

"Supposedly she killed her lover and then herself after learning he had another woman. According to legend, she's still haunting the place, though no one bothered to tell me that until after I'd moved in.''

"So have you ever seen her around?'' he asked.

Suzanne shook her head. "I thought I did once, but, no, I don't really think so.''

For the next hour they talked about everything and nothing, hitting on every subject imaginable except the one that had separated them and then brought them back together. Hart controlled the course of their conversation, steering it in the exact direction he wanted it to go. Finally he brought up a long-ago trip he'd made to Paris.

"I really enjoyed it,'' he said, and smiled. "Of course, I did all the touristy things—visited the Eiffel Tower and the Louvre, dined in sidewalk cafés and cruised the Seine.''

"All of which, unfortunately, I don't have time for when I go,'' Suzanne said.

He feigned surprise. "I didn't realize that your business took you to Europe.''

"Occasionally. England and Paris have a lot to offer in the way of antiques and art. In fact, I just came back from a trip to Paris.''

"Oh?''

She nodded. "It was a buying trip. A young couple who are friends of Clyde's wanted to get rid of some things they'd inherited. Clyde was in the midst of negotiating a rather important private sale and his friends were in a hurry, so I went.'' She sighed. "Their place is a lovely old villa in the country, but of course, I couldn't really enjoy it as much as I'd have liked because I was too busy trying to catalog paintings, furnishings and several trunks loaded with bric-a-brac from what seemed just about every era known to man.''

"Sounds like you've found yourself an interesting career." Friends. And a villa in the country. That would explain her ''disappearance'' after she'd gotten off the plane in Paris. It might even explain the package she'd mailed back there upon her return to the States. It could have contained receipts, payment or appraisal records.

Or stolen plans, an ugly little voice of suspicion whispered.

She smiled. "I enjoy it, though I still have a lot to learn. Clyde can appraise something in a few minutes by just looking at it. I have to carry along a ton of reference books and look everything up."

It was a good story. Maybe it was even true, Hart thought. Nevertheless, it wasn't good enough to risk putting his trust in her. There were still too many unanswered questions, too many possible variables that weren't good.

They finished dinner, both seeming to strive at keeping the accompanying conversation light and impersonal. But the more they talked, the less they really said. He wasn't finding out anything useful, but with each passing minute he was losing more of himself to her.

Suzanne felt the strain that had begun to edge their conversation. It was as if they were both tense and waiting for something. But she didn't know what.

"I never meant to leave without saying good-bye," she said. It had been something she'd thought about ever since the day she'd climbed into her car and driven away from Three Hills, away from Hart, but she hadn't intended to say it aloud. A hot wave of color swept over her cheeks.

The comment surprised him. "I always figured you'd call when you were ready."

She nodded, looking into her coffee, unable to meet his eyes.

"Guess you just never were."

The waiter appeared, refilled their coffee cups and silently departed. Hart was physically and emotionally frustrated, and running out of patience.

"Suzanne."

She gave a slight start, taken back by the sudden chill in his tone.

"Why did you ask Rick for a divorce just before that last mission?" The question surprised him as much as it obviously did her. He'd intended to ask why she'd stolen the files.

Suzanne stared at him. Shock rendered her speechless. It was not only the abrupt change in conversation, but the very question itself.

Beneath the table Hart's fingers closed around his cloth napkin, then clenched into a fist as the old anger returned, sweeping through him like a prairie fire out of control, moving to consume him. He let it—welcomed it. "You know how dangerous, how deadly emotional upheaval can be to a pilot, Suzanne. Especially one about to go on a mission." His tone was accusatory now and edged with condemnation. An image of Rick's Cobra, exploding and plummeting to the ground, flashed through Hart's mind. "Dammit, Suzanne. Why'd you do it?"

She felt every molecule in her body scream a denial of his words. Anger, resentment and hurt rushed through her, stabbing hatefully at her heart.

Rick had fully intended to place the blame for the failure of their marriage on her. The realization of that made her wish more fervently than ever that he was still alive so that she could confront him and slap his face.

She'd suspected him of having several affairs during their marriage, even one with the wife of one of his best friends. But she'd never confronted him, because as much as she'd wanted to, she had always been too afraid it wasn't the right time, that he'd be called out on a mission, that he'd explode in anger and...

The spot on her cheek where Rick had once slapped her suddenly burned, as if the memory of his assault also brought back the pain and humiliation of it.

She stared at Hart as he waited for an answer. She'd known her husband had never been able to stand looking bad in the eyes of his friends, especially Hart's. Now she wondered just how far Rick would have gone, or had gone, to make her the villain of their breakup. Had he even said that she'd been the one having the affairs?

Tears stung her eyes, but she blinked them away, determined not to cry.

"It wasn't like that," she said finally. Fury at Rick churned through her, but it wasn't alone. How could Hart believe that of her? That she would have purposely and carelessly put her own husband's life—anyone's life—in danger?

"It never is," Hart snapped coldly. He signaled the waiter for their check. He'd wanted an explanation, not a halfhearted denial. Something that would convince him he wasn't playing the part of a fool. He stared into her eyes, searching for answers.

He'd known her barely a year before Rick's death, and most of what he knew about her was from what Rick had told him.

And from his own fantasies.

Which meant he didn't really know much of anything.

But how well had Rick known her before marrying her? Or after?

He reined in his runaway emotions and thoughts. "I'm sorry," he said, seeing the anger in her eyes and sensing the wariness toward him that had returned. He'd blundered, maybe irrevocably. Accusations weren't the way to get an enemy to open up. He should be trying to win her trust, not alienate her. Forget mentioning the missing files now, unless he wanted to make things worse. "I don't know why I said that."

"Because it's what you believe of me," Suzanne said softly.

"No." But the look on her face, in her eyes, told him he could deny it forever, and it wouldn't change anything. There was a rift between them now that hadn't been there before. Dammit. He was an idiot. For all the training he'd gone through, the interrogation techniques he'd learned, the subtle ways of getting information from an enemy and gaining their trust, he'd just blown it big time with Suzanne.

"There are always two sides to a story," he said, trying again. Could she really be a spy? A murderer?

He didn't want the answer to be yes, but he knew the possibility was all too real.

"We fell out of love," Suzanne said simply. It was as much of the truth as she was willing to give him now, and at the moment she felt it was far more than he probably deserved to hear.

"It happens," Hart said, continuing the effort to smooth over his blunder. He shrugged. "I just never thought it would happen to you two." She could have used wifely concern to subtly pump Rick for information, then passed it on to an accomplice, maybe another member of the corps, someone who'd sabotaged Rick's chopper and stolen the secret plans for the weapons-detection device.

It made too much sense, and he hated that.

They went outside, but instead of heading toward the parking lot, Hart steered Suzanne toward the vast garden that surrounded Cactus Jack's. "I'm sorry," he said again. "I said things I shouldn't have a while ago. I don't even know why I did. I know you wouldn't have purposely hurt Rick."

She nodded. "You were his best friend," Suzanne said.

Her response surprised him, set him back a moment. Then he decided it was most likely just another attempt to garner his sympathy and cooperation.

They walked on in silence.

Moonlight touched the landscape, weaving its way in and about the tall cacti, the wild grasses and well-tended roses, competing with the flames that danced atop the ends of the torches set strategically around the garden and creating a canvas of light and shadow.

Hart noticed that it also gently touched Suzanne's hair, turned some strands to cascading waves of fire and others to infinite darkness; it danced within her eyes, caressed her bare shoulders and shimmered along the lines of the simple white dress she wore.

Heaven help him, in spite of everything that had happened, in spite of his anger, his frustrations, his resentment, even his suspicions, he still wanted her with a desperation that was almost killing him. Desire had been building in him ever since the moment she'd walked back into his life, gnawing at him like a hungry flame, threatening his self-control and instinct for survival.

What was there about Suzanne Cassidy that made him forget the need for caution? That urged him to pull her into his arms and damn the consequences and danger?

"How can something so beautiful be so deceptive and deadly?" Suzanne said as she stared out at the desert.

Hart's gaze moved over her, his thoughts stopped by her words, momentarily mistaking them for a confession.

"So many lethal creatures live out there," Suzanne said, "yet you can look at the desert at times like this and see nothing but beauty."

She looked back when he didn't respond, and as their eyes met and their gazes locked, Hart saw innocence. He knew it could be nothing more than a lie, like the desert's facade of safety. Nevertheless, the desire to pull her into his arms was almost overpowering.

Cursing under his breath, he drew on every ounce of emotional strength he possessed and reminded himself he was engaged in a war unlike any he'd ever fought. She was his enemy, at least until proven otherwise.

From the day he'd realized his mother had abandoned him, Hart had kept the core of his emotions, the essence of himself, locked away, taking what he'd wanted from life and giving back as little as possible. That was exactly what he intended to do now.

He didn't believe in love—never had and never would—but he did believe in desire. And in war, it was as good a tool as any other.

And this was definitely war.

Suzanne knew that trying to look away from his eyes was impossible. She tried anyway, feeling a sudden need to escape, and failed.

For one brief second it seemed every hard, unyielding line of him resonated with rage, all directed at her. The cold contempt in his eyes, the animosity she'd felt come over him sporadically ever since she'd returned, the resentment that seemed to exude from him. She saw it all now. The sight chilled her to the bone. At the same time she found herself unerringly drawn to him, searingly aware of the virility and force that surrounded him and beckoned to her.

Fear and want battled for control of her. She wanted to tear her gaze from his, to turn back the way she'd come and race through the garden until she was far away from him. But she couldn't.

Suddenly he closed the distance between them and pulled her into his arms.

A soft shriek of surprise slipped from Suzanne's throat.

Play the game, Hart told himself. Play the game. His lips crashed down on hers, giving Suzanne no chance to turn away or refuse him, demanding she give, while all he intended to do was take.

His arms tightened around her, crushing her to him until her curves melded with his lines, until there was no light, no air, between them, only the thin veil of their clothes.

Other women had aroused his passions, stoked and satisfied his desires, but none had threatened his self-control the way Suzanne did.

Was she the essence of all his dreams or the reality of all his nightmares? He didn't know, couldn't decide and at the moment didn't care.

Play the game! a voice in the back of his mind screamed again. The game. But the sound that penetrated his desires and reached his consciousness was barely a whisper, too faint to be noticed.

His hands were splayed on her back, and he could feel the fragileness of her bones as he caressed her, the raggedness of her breath as he continued to incite her passion, the rapid beat of her heart as she surrendered to what they both wanted.

He slid a hand upward, his fingers delving into the long tendrils of her hair and losing themselves within that silky darkness.

''Hart,'' she whispered, her voice ragged with emotion.

His name on her lips was a caress he couldn't resist, a whispering stroke of seduction that pulled him over the edge and banished any thread of reason left to him.

The game plan was forgotten as if it had never existed.

He wanted her with an intensity that gave him no choice, needed her the way he needed air to breathe.

Suzanne felt as if she was losing herself to him, as if all her will and reason, everything in her that was Suzanne Cassidy, was being devoured by the passion he was stirring to fiery life within her.

She had tried to hold herself back from him; told herself when she'd returned to Three Hills that it was only to gain his help, to find the truth behind the FBI's suspicions and allegations. There had been nothing between her and Hart before, and there was nothing between them now except friendship, if that.

But it had been a lie. It had always been a lie.

Her senses leaped to life at his touch, then burned with need. It had never been like this with Rick. So intense. Theirs had been a quiet love, so quiet that when it began to die neither realized it until it was gone. A delicious shiver raced through her body as his tongue slid into her mouth and danced and dueled about hers. The heat of his body enveloped and invaded her own like a rampaging fire, and a pulsing, hungry, demanding, knot of desire formed deep inside of her.

It wasn't supposed to be this way between them, but it was, and she knew there was nothing she could do to stop it.

She tightened her arms around his neck, and her body pressed more urgently against his.

Hart's lips were hard and searching, his passion commanding her own to respond, the fire of his needs melding with hers.

His passion stoked her desire.

Her desire fired his passion.

It was an intimacy like none Suzanne had ever known, an invasion of feeling she had never expected to experience, had not been aware even existed.

She knew her surrender to him was inevitable. Maybe she'd always known that. She suddenly jerked out of his arms, the ugly thought racing through her mind and sobering her like a bucket of cold water. Was that why they'd chosen her to frame? How whoever was behind this thing had done it? By using her attraction to Hart?

Chapter 7

The ringing of the phone startled Suzanne out of her dreams of Hart. She hurried across the room and snatched up the receiver, half hoping it was him, yet dreading the prospect that it was.

She wanted to hear his voice...and wanted time to convince herself that what had happened between them, what she'd felt when in his arms, had meant nothing.

"Suzanne?"

Relief. Disappointment. Joy. Dread. "Hi, Mom," Suzanne forced past a stifled groan.

"I tried your cell phone, honey, but it didn't work."

Because Suzanne had it plugged in to recharge.

"So I called Clyde. He gave me this number. I just had to talk to you."

Suzanne adored her mother, but there was only one reason Lyla Ramsey-Conners-Ponder-Njorney-

Houston-Bracci-Drake ever called her only daughter in the middle of the night. It was a conversation they'd had numerous times, and one Suzanne didn't welcome.

When she got back to L.A., she'd hang Clyde from the ceiling by his toes for giving her mother the number to the bungalow.

"Joey and I broke up," Lyla said. An exaggerated sigh followed. "I'm afraid it's over between us."

Big surprise, Suzanne thought, although this marriage had lasted six months longer than her mother's last three. "I'm sorry," Suzanne said, just as she always did. "Are you all right?"

"Oh, yes, I'm fine. But it was inevitable, I guess," Lyla said. "We were just too different."

Before Suzanne could respond, her mother began to expound on all the reasons she and her latest husband were going their separate ways.

Half an hour later, lost in thoughts of Hart while her mother continued to talk, Suzanne heard her finally say she had to go or she'd look like a zombie when she met her attorney in the morning.

Suzanne refrained from asking if he was a marital prospect, told her mother to take care and hung up. After fixing herself a cup of coffee, she walked out onto the patio and sat on the chaise longue.

The night was still warm, the sky like a velvet black blanket sprinkled with diamonds. A sliver of moon hung above the distant mountains, while the desert's uniquely sultry scent permeated the air.

How could she have responded to Hart's kiss like that? She knew she couldn't trust him, knew he could be... She chased the thought away and forced her mind to the problem of why she'd come to Three Hills.

They'd found no blemish whatsoever on anyone's record, neither corps members nor family members, but Suzanne knew blemishes could be concealed. The secret plans had disappeared during the mission, and that had to mean that someone directly connected to the Cobra Corps, if not Hart, was guilty.

She didn't see any other possibility. But she wanted to. She desperately wanted to.

Hart sat in his Cobra and stared up at the night sky, not really seeing it. Instead, he saw Suzanne, tasted her lips crushed to his, felt the heat of her body, the touch of her flesh. He was losing the battle to find the truth and losing himself—again—to her.

He gripped the stick, squeezing down hard. Sitting in the Cobra, being alone and hearing the silence or flying through the sky, the rotor blades singing overhead, had always helped him find the answers he sought. But not tonight. Nothing was working tonight.

Frustrated and angry with himself, he climbed from the chopper, stalked across the tarmac to his car and drove back to his apartment. Maybe sleep would help, if he could get any. He pushed open the front door, flipped on the light switch as he stepped inside—and cursed.

He strode from room to room, glaring at one slightly disturbed object after another, as if it could tell him, and wouldn't, who had been in his home and rifled, ever so carefully, but not quite carefully enough, through his things.

The feds. The accusation popped into his mind

instantly. It was their style. No up-front questions, no warrants. Just go in, look for and, if necessary, take what they wanted. He opened, then slammed drawers shut, grabbed a pillow from the sofa, put it back, picked it up again and threw it halfway across the room.

He wanted it to be the feds. Told himself it had to have been the feds. But there was another possibility, one he didn't like: Suzanne. He'd left her hours ago, and whether he wanted to believe it or not, it could just as easily have been her who'd gone through his things.

Anger seared him—at them, at her, at himself. If he'd come home after leaving her, there wouldn't have been an opportunity for anyone to break in. He looked around again. What had they been looking for?

Then another thought struck him. Maybe they hadn't been looking for something so much as planting something. His anger turned to alarm. Had something been left in his apartment that would make him appear guilty of treason? Something that would point to him as a thief and murderer?

Cops, MPs…could have been called and be on the way to his apartment right now.

He began searching through drawers and closets for anything that shouldn't be there. When he found nothing, he began to search again, but this time he looked for bugs or hidden cameras under tables, chairs and inside lamps and the phone.

Again he came up with nothing, except the realization that sleep wasn't going to come to him anytime soon. He switched on his computer. He'd placed a call to the senator earlier, but the man's secretary claimed that Trowtin was out of town. And he hadn't returned the call yet. Hart pulled up his e-mail. The senator hadn't answered that, either. It was as if he'd fallen off the face of the earth or turned incommunicado. At least where Hart was concerned.

He remembered Suzanne's saying her partner's name was Clyde Weller. Hart punched in the name and clicked on "search."

The next morning when the phone rang, Hart felt as if a saw was slicing through his head. His temples throbbed, a spot between his eyes ached—even his brain felt as if it hurt, and images of Suzanne filled his mind. Groaning, disgusted with himself, he rolled over and grabbed the phone, more to stop its ringing than respond to the caller.

His life was spiraling into an abyss of disaster, and all he could do was dream about making love to the woman who could very well be the one who'd pushed him into it.

"Sir," Private Roubechard said, "Company Commander Lewis has requested that you be in his office in one hour."

The aide's words immediately chased any lingering shadows of sleep from Hart's body and, for the moment, all thought of Suzanne from his mind. But his head continued to pound. He normally didn't drink, and spiking that last cup of coffee while he'd been on the computer last night obviously had not been a good idea. "I'll be there," he said, and hung up. He had no doubt what was happening to him. He just didn't know how to stop it.

Three cups of strong coffee and three aspirins

later, he made it to the base, reporting to the commander's office ten minutes early.

"At ease, Captain," Major Lewis said, looking up from the files he'd been reading through on his desk as Hart entered and saluted. Lewis removed his glasses and rubbed the crest of his blunt nose between thumb and forefinger. "I'll be brief and to the point, Captain," he said, leveling his piercing blue gaze at Hart. "I received another request for your 201 file this morning, and this time I was ordered not to deny it. I don't know why Washington is so interested in you or why they want the file. I don't even know who actually requested it. But I wanted to inform you of this morning's events in person. Your file has been sent to the Pentagon."

Hart nodded, while his stomach plunged to the floor. "Thank you, sir." He was running out of time.

Lewis stared at him. "For what?" he asked gruffly. "If I were in your shoes, I sure wouldn't be thanking someone for sending my file to Washington."

Five minutes later Hart stood before Roubechard's desk, anger and more than a little alarm and fear niggling at his nerves. "Do whatever you have to do to get it done, Private, but I want Suzanne Cassidy's phone tapped, and I want it done now. I also want another background check on her, and this time I want to know everything there is to know about the lady. Go all the way back to the very second she was born if you have to. Whatever."

Hart stalked into his office, then immediately turned around and walked back out. "Roubechard, track down everyone who had even the remotest connection to the corps last year. Put special emphasis on anyone and anything connected to the Jaguar Loop mission. Get detailed personnel reports on all of them. And get the autopsy report on Rick Cassidy.'' He slammed the door and walked to his desk. If the FBI suspected him, Rick and Suzanne of treason, then he knew they weren't looking any further. Which meant if he didn't want to end up wearing leg irons and looking at the world through barred windows for the rest of his life, he had to.

He glanced at the clock on his desk. It was barely 9:00 a.m. If he hurried, maybe he could get to her place before she had breakfast.

''Sir?'' Roubechard said, as Hart stormed past him toward the exit door.

''What?'' he growled, stopping.

''I, uh, just wanted to remind you, sir, that the base's annual open house starts in two hours, and you're due on the field.''

''Today?''

''Yes, sir.''

Hart cursed under his breath. He'd forgotten, which meant he didn't have time to take Suzanne to breakfast, but he would have to go to his apartment and pick up a dress uniform. Maybe he'd have time to swing by her place and invite her to the open house.

His life was mired in disaster, and he was supposed to smile and give a flight exhibition.

Hart climbed from his chopper and, after talking to a few children at the edge of the tarmac, walked toward the hangar, where he'd arranged to meet Suzanne.

The second batch of background checks he'd ordered were being held up—red tape, a clerk in Personnel had said. Hart couldn't get past the suspicion that just maybe someone was purposely holding things up. And getting a copy of Rick's autopsy report was beginning to look even less promising. The request had been flat-out denied. That had stirred his curiosity, to say nothing of his suspicions, and made him want to look at it all the more. So he'd called Major Lewis and, saying only that Rick's wife wanted to see it and he didn't really know why, asked him to request a copy.

He still hadn't heard back from the senator, and when he'd called again, just before coming out to the field, the secretary had explained that the senator was "out of town and couldn't be reached."

Hart was starting to wonder if the man was avoiding him. A dispiriting thought.

He spotted Suzanne right away standing near one of the huge hangars that housed the Cobra Corps choppers. Her dark hair glistened richly beneath the hot afternoon sun, like dark strands of silk touched by flame, contrasting starkly with the sleeveless white blouse she wore tucked into a pair of cutoffs. The outfit was simple, and one he'd seen on hundreds of other women, but on her it was a seductive draping of cloth that drew his eyes to the tantalizing curves of her body, down the length of her long, bare, perfectly shaped legs, and nearly took his breath away.

For a brief moment, as their gazes locked across the tarmac, it was as if they'd never met. As if all the pain and tragedy in their combined pasts didn't exist and they were strangers, meeting for the first time, attracted to each other, with no reason to think the other was anything more or less than what they seemed.

But they weren't strangers, he reminded himself. The pain and tragedy of their pasts was all too real. And all too ugly, if his and the FBI's suspicions were right.

Secret plans had been stolen, and Rick was dead. Cold, hard facts Hart couldn't deny.

Suzanne smiled and waved to him.

Welcome to my web, said the spider to the fly. The thought instantly flashed through his mind. He tried to push it aside, but it remained, dark and ugly. He knew he couldn't let his guard down; he had to be wary of her.

He walked toward her, smiling, and was halfway across the tarmac when Chief Carger appeared from within the hangar and approached Suzanne from behind.

"Mrs. Cassidy, nice to see you again."

Suzanne turned. The uneasiness she'd once felt around him swept over her again as she looked into his eyes. "Oh, hello, Chief."

He glanced toward Hart and frowned. "You being careful, Mrs. Cassidy?" he said.

She followed his gaze, instantly put off by the implication in his words. "I'm fine, Chief," she said coolly. "Please don't worry yourself over me."

Carger nodded. "Don't mean to interfere where I'm not wanted, but one thing a lady like you ought to remember…" He glanced back at Hart. "The captain's a warrior. Always will be." He shoved a cigarette between his lips. "Man like that likes the danger of putting his life on the line, day in, day out.''

She frowned. Why was he telling her this?

"You should stay away from him," the chief said, as if reading her mind. "You deserve better."

"We're friends, Chief, that's all," Suzanne said, then wondered why she'd felt the need to explain anything to the man. It was none of his business if she and Hart were friends, enemies or passionate lovers.

A heat rushed through her as her last thought brought an image of Hart to her mind, of his body pressed to hers, his arms crushing her to him, his lips ravaging hers, stirring her passions, routing her senses.

She turned away from the chief and looked back at Hart. The heat instantly intensified, an avalanche of fire, consuming her and sending a hot shiver dancing over her skin. Her reactions to Hart were insane and irresponsible, but she couldn't help them. She watched him close the distance between them, saw the coldness in his eyes as they settled on the chief and wondered at it. Was there a problem between the two men? Or was it exactly the opposite? Was the chief Hart's accomplice?

Was it possible that rather than just running into her, the chief was really watching her?

The chief saluted Hart. "You're needed on the far runway," Hart said. "Rand thinks his chopper has an oil leak." It wasn't true, but he didn't care. He just wanted the man to leave.

Hart watched the chief walk away, wondering at his own actions. Why did he feel such anger toward Carger? What did he care if the man talked to Suzanne, unless it was more than just casual or even flirtatious conversation? Could Carger be her contact? Her accomplice?

The man had been on the Jaguar Loop mission.

"You were wonderful up there," Suzanne said, referring to the flight exercise his squad had just performed for the open-house audience and interrupting Hart's suspicious speculation.

For months after Rick's death she'd never wanted to see another helicopter for as long as she lived. But she'd finally come to realize that, as unfortunate as it was, Rick had died doing what he loved.

"I wasn't sure you'd come." The moment he heard his own words, Hart wished he hadn't said them. Whether she'd come or not shouldn't have mattered to him, and he didn't want her to think it did.

"I wouldn't have missed it," she said softly. She glanced past him at the Cobras sitting on the far runway. "Would you take me up sometime?"

Hart stared at her. None of the women he'd dated had ever asked to be taken up in his Cobra. Even if someone had, the answer would have been no. But now the question coming from Suzanne pulled at something in him, made him want to say yes, and made him want her more desperately than ever.

The question surprised Suzanne as much as it obviously did him. Why had she asked that? She'd never wanted to go up in one of the things before—especially after Rick's death. But now the thought of being in a helicopter with Hart—just the two of them—alone together—in the clouds—

Her gaze met his and she felt her breath slip quietly but quickly from her lungs. The look of longing she saw in his eyes was so intense, so dark and alluring, it was a shock to her entire system.

"Whenever you want," he said, the unique drawl of his deep voice wrapping around her like a velvet cloak, brushing her skin and caressing her senses. A slow smile tugged at the corners of his mouth, and the beckoning call of his eyes intensified, pulling at her.

The masculine force of him was like nothing she'd ever felt, an aura of strength and purpose that seemed nearly tangible.

It wasn't supposed to be this way between them. It wasn't why she'd come back. Her mind told her heart to turn away from him, ignore him, beware of him, and her heart refused to listen. Caution had deserted her.

Suzanne's gaze moved over him, searching, yet she didn't really know what it was she was searching for.

The sun shone golden off each wave of his hair, played within the deep blue of his eyes and created shadows about the rugged lines of his face.

She wanted to reach out and touch him, feel the smoothness of his cheek beneath her hand, trace her fingertips along the line of that strong, granitelike jaw, press them to the slash of lips that had proved to have the gentlest touch she'd ever felt.

Hart was all too aware of the fine line he was walking and that his control was on the very edge, carefully balanced and not at all infallible. But at the moment, that concern wasn't a high priority.

Suzanne's breath stalled in her throat. She knew what he was going to do, knew it was wrong, that she should turn away...and knew it was too late.

She had neither the will nor the strength. Maybe she never had.

She watched his hand move toward her, felt it touch her neck, like a searing brand she would never forget, never cease to feel, then slip to her nape. He slowly drew her to him, his eyes boring into hers as his head lowered toward her.

Every nerve in her body was tense with anticipation, and at the same time, she was calmer than she'd ever been in her life. The scent of his aftershave, a light, airy redolence, surrounded Suzanne and reminded her of blue skies and white clouds, of cool wind and summer rain.

His breath touched her cheek, a gentle caress that sent a shiver coursing through her.

She leaned into his touch.

Desire darkened his eyes.

His lips brushed over hers, lightly, lingering for just a second—yet it seemed the most erotic, most intense kiss she'd ever experienced. Her body felt as if it had melted, the strength in her bones, in her muscles, having disappeared. All thought of caution and fear left her, and all the barriers she'd tried to erect around her heart began to crumble and fall aside.

"Hart," she said, struggling to pull air into her lungs, to speak over the deafening beat of her heart. "We really shouldn't...I mean..." Her body was tingling with want of him. "This isn't a good idea."

"I know." His mouth captured hers, this kiss deeper, more demanding. She felt his arms wrap around her, draw her to him, crush her body to his.

It felt so good. So right.

The crowds of people on the tarmac, only a short

distance away, were forgotten. The only reality left
to Suzanne was Hart, his lips stirring her passion,
his body arousing her desire, his arms holding her
tight, safe, home.

She had waited so long.

Suddenly Hart's beeper sounded.

He watched from the hangar, just out of their
sight, yet within full view of everyone else. Damn
Hart Branson. Everything had been going so well
until he'd entered the picture. But that was her fault.
Hers and the fault of that damned FBI agent who
wouldn't let it go. Cross every t, dot every i. That
was his type. And now he had this situation to con-
tend with. Branson was getting too close and was
going to ruin everything if they didn't stop him.

Several people walked by, laughing, talking about
the exhibits, the aerial maneuvers, the pilots. A teenager stopped to ask a question. He answered it, af-
fably, but he never took his eyes off Hart and Suzanne.

Tension ate at his nerves, and that fueled his anger. He'd been right, but then he'd known he was.
He had guessed she would come back here, would
plead with Branson to help her. But the others had
argued that Suzanne would never come back to
Three Hills. And they'd been wrong.

DeBraggo walked casually around one of the exhibition Cobras, all the while keeping Suzanne, the
major and the other man watching them within his
sight. He pulled on one end of the fake mustache
he'd pasted to his upper lip, yanked down on the

brim of his baseball cap, and repositioned his dark glasses on his nose.

There were too many players entering the game, and at the moment he wasn't sure who was watching who.

Suzanne paced the length of her living room, stared out the glass doors at the night-shrouded desert, then turned and paced toward the opposite side of the room.

It was too late now. He wasn't going to call. But it didn't matter. It was good that he hadn't called. What had happened between them, what was happening between them, was a mistake. Maybe a dangerous one for her.

For probably the hundredth time since he'd left her by the hangar to answer a page, she called herself a fool. Coming to Hart for help had been the wrong thing to do. Whatever she felt for him, and it obviously wasn't fear or even wariness, her traitorous emotions could cloud her judgment. If that happened, she just might pay for it with her life.

She fixed herself another cup of coffee, stood at the sliding glass door that led to the patio and stared out at the night.

Why didn't he call?

She ate a half-dozen chocolate-chip cookies, drank another cup of coffee and paced the length of the room.

Where was he? She ate more cookies and drank another cup of coffee. Finally she told herself she was being foolish. It was time to get some sleep, stop thinking about Hart Branson and stop imagining everyone was out to get her.

Suzanne turned off the living-room lights, checked the doors to make certain they were locked and walked into her bedroom. A good night's sleep would calm her nerves and maybe give her a fresh perspective on things. She opened the armoire to get her negligee and her heart nearly burst from her chest. A shriek of dismay ripped from her throat.

Several of her garments lay on the floor.

Someone had been in the bungalow.

She stared at a pale yellow silk blouse she'd carefully hung up when she'd unpacked several days ago. Its breast pocket was turned inside out.

Suzanne spun around, her gaze darting about the room. Everything had seemed okay when she'd come in here earlier, but then she really hadn't been paying attention—she'd only stayed in the bedroom long enough to toss her bag and jacket on the bed. Now, as she looked closer, she realized things were slightly askew, as if someone had methodically searched through everything and tried to leave things exactly as they'd found them.

But they hadn't. She grabbed a silver-plated hand mirror from the dresser and, clutching it tightly in her fist, held it up to use as a weapon, if need be.

Silence surrounded her, except for the soft sounds of the desert drifting in through the open window, which hadn't been open earlier.

Had she interrupted their search when she'd returned? Had they slipped out the back door as she'd entered the front?

Her gaze darted around the room again. Someone could be under the bed. Behind the bathroom door. ''Oh, God,'' she whimpered, too scared to even move.

No sound responded.

No, they were gone. Most likely whoever it had been had left through the window when they'd heard her enter the house. A thread of relief offered itself to her. Who would have done this? Her mind raced in search of an answer. It couldn't have been Hart, because she'd been with him.

But not all day, a little voice in the back of her mind whispered. He'd had to leave—remember?

After he'd been paged she had stayed at the base for another two hours, enjoying the exhibits and talking to some of the other pilots, the mechanics, even a recruiter. She knew Hart had flown another exercise for the open house and had spent some time answering questions for some of the visitors. But then he'd disappeared.

She was reading something into nothing.

Or was she?

She ran to the phone, grabbed the receiver from its cradle, then instantly slammed it down again.

It might not have been Hart, but it could have been an accomplice. One who'd come here while Hart was at the base, one who'd searched through her things while Hart had pulled her into his arms and kissed her until all she'd been able to think about was how much she wanted him.

By the time Hart got back to his apartment, the sun had long ago disappeared beyond the horizon, and he was bone weary and exhausted. The day had been full, and had gotten even fuller after General Walthorp had paged him. The general's own squad captain had taken suddenly ill, so the general had brusquely ordered Hart to head a flight exercise of Blackhawks for the open house.

Chief Carger had been the gunner on the Blackhawk Hart flew. That had grated on his nerves, and he didn't know why. He'd always gotten along well with the chief in the past.

Hart remembered seeing him with Suzanne and feeling angry, but he knew that was caused by suspicion, nothing more. Someone connected with the corps, whether he liked it or not, was guilty of treason and betrayal, and the chief was just as good a possibility as anyone else.

After the exercise he'd been interviewed by several media reps, then spent what seemed like hours answering questions from visitors. He'd finally been able to hand the stage over to Cowboy when he was paged again.

He glanced at the phone and thought about calling Suzanne, then decided against it. His desire to talk to her had nothing to do with the investigation.

Hart sighed and lay down on his bed, not even bothering to remove his clothes and forcing his thoughts away from Suzanne.

Major Lewis had called him into his office, congratulated him for his team's part in the success of the open house and thanked him for taking on the extra duty for Walthorp. Then he'd given him the bad news. Someone from Washington had called again. This time they were asking questions about his personal life.

Hart had laughed. On that point there wasn't much to tell. His personal life was practically nil.

Except for Suzanne.

He ignored the whisper that floated up from his

subconscious, rolled over and buried his face in his pillow.

An hour later the fact that he was not falling asleep was undeniable. He sat up, moved to his desk and flipped on the computer.

The first thing he saw was that he had a message from the senator.

Hart cursed himself for not checking his e-mail earlier and brought the message onto the screen.

"Do NOT make any more inquiries regarding Jaguar Loop, and do not trust ANYONE."

Chapter 8

"I got your e-mail, Senator," Hart said. The anxiety he'd been fighting to control all day suddenly intensified. This was the fourth time in less than half an hour he'd tried to reach the senator, and the secretary had finally put him through.

"Good. Hope you understood it, Captain."

"Not completely, sir. But..." He filled Senator Trowtin in on what was happening. "I need to know exactly what evidence the feds have for suspecting Suzanne Cassidy of treason and possible murder, sir."

"They suspect you, too, Captain," the senator said, his voice gruff, his tone almost accusatory. "Don't forget that."

"No, sir, I haven't. But I was hoping you could tell me—"

"No, Captain," the senator said, cutting him off. "I'm afraid I can't. Sorry."

The line went dead.

Hart stared at the phone, surprised at what had just happened and knowing he shouldn't be. Someone had gotten to the senator. But who? And how? He cursed, shot from his chair, paced the room, slammed a drawer, thought of throwing something through the window, then sat down again. It didn't matter who'd gotten to him or what kind of threat they'd used. They'd gotten to him. The man was obviously frightened, probably with good reason, and he wasn't going to help anymore. End of story.

Hart dialed Suzanne's number, then hung up before her phone rang.

He called his commanding officer and got another evasive response. But he knew Major Lewis would do what he could, anyway.

Five phone calls and several long hours later he'd called in all the favors he could remember and was trying to decide on his next move when a knock sounded on his door, and Roubechard opened it. "Excuse me, sir, but I thought you'd want to know what I've found."

Hart motioned him to enter and the aide approached his desk.

"Ms. Cassidy's cousin and business partner, Clyde Weller…"

"Yes?" Hart said, his patience strained.

"Well, sir, it appears he's had several questionable associates in the past, sir. His ex-fiancée's brother is Antony Giani."

Hart recognized the name of the well-known mob boss the government had finally been able to make a case against two years ago.

"Mr. Weller's mother was once married to Senator Rollstad."

Who'd been involved in a payback scandal, Hart recalled.

"And Robert Marsei is a customer of the gallery Weller owns with Ms. Cassidy."

The infamous French spy.

"Terrific," Hart snarled softly, more to himself than Roubechard.

"She spoke with Mr. Marsei last night, sir. He said the payment had been transferred, and he expected his goods delivered within the next two days."

"Check the airlines, Roubechard," Hart said, grabbing his car keys and standing. "See if she's flying out. Or if her business partner has booked himself a trip out of the States." He'd tried every variation of the name *Weller* he could think of while searching the Net and had come up with nothing. But that didn't really mean anything. A lot of people used aliases when doing things they shouldn't be doing.

"What about Ms. Cassidy's mother, sir?"

"Check her out, too. And his," Hart said. "And check out her stepfathers. Probably a wild-goose chase, but you never know." He grabbed one of the office's cell phones on his way out the door. "I've got number five," he said, holding up the phone. "Call me when you get something."

He hurried around to the side of the building and climbed into his car. Dammit to hell, enough was enough. It was long past time to lay it all on the line with her. He'd been putting this off—telling himself he'd need more answers first, but that had only been an excuse. He was trained in POW interrogation, of knowing how to read a person, how to get them to tell you what you wanted to know. Either she was innocent and he'd be able to tell, or she was guilty as sin.

That last thought sent his heart plummeting.

He sped off the base.

She was going to give him answers this time.

Twenty minutes later he turned the corner that led onto her street and Suzanne's bungalow came into sight.

A man was standing on her porch.

Hart hastily swerved the Vette to the curb, pulled in behind a yellow Volkswagen Beetle and cut the engine. A large, white artificial daisy was attached to the Beetle's antenna.

He silently ordered the man talking to Suzanne to turn so he could see his face. But when he did, Hart was shocked.

What in blazes was Carger doing at Suzanne's place? Hart mulled the question over in his mind as he watched them.

Anger, hot and sudden, exploded within him when he saw the chief lean over and kiss her.

Was he her accomplice? Her lover? The thought filled him with disgust and threatened to rip control of his temper from his tight grip. Carger had been at Jaguar Loop. A gunner for one of the supporting Blackhawks and the squad's crew chief and head mechanic. He could have stolen the plans and he could have easily sabotaged Rick's Cobra. And he would know who to talk to, who to tip off, to get an investigation going into another soldier's record if he wanted to get suspicion off himself.

* * *

"I don't understand," Suzanne said, uneasy beneath what she recognized as a very assessing gaze. He was standing too close, the look in his eyes too blatantly sexual and threatening, and he was talking nonsense. She had never been comfortable around him, even those nights he'd been at the house with Rick and some others, which was why now she hadn't invited him inside when she'd opened the door and found him standing on her doorstep. And she didn't like the fact that Hart's aide had told him where she was staying. She'd have to mention that to Hart—and ask him to tell Roubechard not to do that again.

"I just thought, if you didn't already know, you should," Chief Carger said. "The captain isn't exactly the kind of man who cares about anything much other than his career. He's stepped on a lot of people to get where he's at, and it's a safe bet in my book he'll be stepping on a whole lot more to get where he wants to go."

She didn't see what the accusation had to do with her. "Chief, I—"

"There's always been talk among the men," the chief said, interrupting her. "Speculation, you know? Especially whenever Captain Branson disappears for a bit."

"What do you mean, disappears?" Suzanne asked, fear and anger fighting for control.

The chief shrugged. "He gets called away."

Her look remained blank.

"His clearance is Cosmic," he said impatiently, as if that should be explanation enough.

It was, and the word sent a wave of icy chills

dancing across Suzanne's skin, leaving it a blanket of goose bumps. She had been an army brat, army clerk and army widow. She knew what the divisions of top-secret clearances were, and she knew that Cosmic was one of the highest. She also knew that it was given only to someone who needed access to NATO plans, war strategies and nuclear information.

Was Hart, like Rick had obviously been, more than what he seemed?

Her knees felt suddenly weak, her world darker than it had been only a moment ago.

"I tried to warn you before," the chief said. "He ain't the kind of man a nice woman like you should get involved with. I like you, Mrs. Cassidy, always have, and I liked Rick. He was a good man. Good soldier. So I just figured you should know about the captain, if you didn't already, and I figured you didn't."

He was right about one thing: she hadn't known about Hart's clearance. But it seemed there had been a lot she hadn't known.

Did it make any difference, though? She smiled, and though she didn't want to, she made herself offer the chief her hand. "Thank you, Chief Carger, I appreciate your concern," she said. When his hand wrapped around hers, Suzanne felt the urge to cringe. Instead, she forced a smile. "But as I told you before, the captain and I are only old friends, that's all."

Liar, a little voice in the back of her mind said.

Before she knew what was happening, the chief bent and pressed his lips to her cheek. "You take care,'' he said softly into her ear, then released her. ''I'd hate to see anything happen to you.''

She gave a start and drew back. The words sounded like mere concern, but something told her they could also be a threat. She looked up and into his eyes, but all she saw in the dark-brown depths was the warmth of his smile.

''If you need anything at all,'' he said, ''you just give me a call.''

She watched him walk to his car, realizing the hair on the back of her neck had risen at his touch. For some reason she couldn't explain even to herself, his comment seemed not so much one of simple concern as a warning.

Suzanne waited until the chief started to drive away before she entered the bungalow. She paused in the kitchen and stared at the phone. She should call Hart, tell him what the chief had said. There might be some reason for the chief having come to her, some reason he'd told her those things other than his ''concern'' for her. She picked up the phone and started to dial Hart's number, then stopped. Was the chief right about Hart? Her own father had been like that—so dedicated to his career that he didn't care who he walked on to get where he wanted to go. It was part of what had destroyed her parents' marriage. That, and Lyla's wandering eye.

She touched a finger to her lips, remembering Hart's kiss.

Suddenly she missed him more than she'd ever missed anyone. She tried to shake the feeling away, but it wouldn't leave. He hadn't called or come by since she'd seen him at the open house, but maybe he had reason. She finished dialing his number, then hung up when Roubechard answered.

She glanced at the clock on the wall over the refrigerator. She would tell Hart what the chief had said, but not over the phone and not now. She had to leave for her appointment in Tucson...should have left fifteen minutes ago. Grabbing her bag and car keys, she ran out to her rental car. If she didn't hurry, she was going to be late.

DeBraggo had seen Hart pull his car up behind the yellow Volkswagen and had watched with interest as the captain watched Suzanne Cassidy talking on the porch with Chief Carger.

He'd wished however, that Suzanne and the chief had gone inside, where the bug he'd planted would have allowed him to overhear their conversation. Maybe he should do a little checking into the chief's personal life.

He sank down in his car seat until completely out of sight when Suzanne drove past, and remained there until he was certain Hart had pulled out and followed her. He had already searched both their residences and found nothing. Though she'd almost caught him in the act while he'd been going through hers. He'd had to climb out the bedroom window when he'd heard her enter the bungalow. He started the dark sedan and pulled away from the curb, swinging the car completely around and heading in the same direction Suzanne and Hart had taken.

Hart turned the corner after Suzanne, hoping she hadn't noticed him behind her. Minutes later they'd traveled through the small downtown of Three Hills and left it behind. The long stretch of highway running through the desert was fairly deserted, so Hart pulled off several times in rest stops so that she wouldn't be suspicious of the same car always being behind her.

He thought he'd noticed the same dark sedan behind him once too often, but it had disappeared about ten minutes ago, so he figured it was merely his imagination.

Unless she was going to someone's ranch or meeting someone on the road, he knew she had to be on her way to Tucson. There weren't any other towns between it and Three Hills.

Meeting someone she couldn't afford anyone in Three Hills to see her with? his suspicious mind asked.

They were approaching the outskirts of Tucson when Hart noticed the dark car was behind him again. He slowed to let it pass. It didn't. He pushed down on the accelerator. It remained behind him. He remembered the car the chief had driven away from Suzanne's. It had been dark, but he hadn't paid any attention to its make or model. Hart swore. If that was the chief behind him, the man was going to be repairing choppers at the North Pole for the next 120 years.

Suzanne drove toward downtown. The streets were crowded with cars and pedestrians, and Hart knew he couldn't lose sight of her. If he did, he probably would never find her again.

He glanced in his rearview mirror. The dark car had pulled off about half a mile back and hadn't reappeared. He chastised himself for imagining a problem where there wasn't one.

Suzanne slowed, then pulled into the parking lot of Laurel Kay's coffee shop.

Hart circled the block, not wanting to pull in directly behind her. By the time he returned, parked and entered the restaurant, Suzanne was seated in a booth toward the back of the spacious restaurant. Another woman sat across from her.

Hart stood at the door and peered past the fronds of a large potted plant that stood there. The woman was about the same age as Suzanne, her hair blond and cut short, her makeup heavily applied. She was pretty, but not strikingly so. Several gold bracelets adorned her right wrist, a watch her left, and a thick gold choker circled her neck. The jewelry looked real and expensive. Everything about her looked expensive.

But something about her made him think he might have seen her somewhere before. If he had, he didn't remember where or when. He saw a waitress eye him curiously. Hart quickly took a seat at the counter. His back was to Suzanne and her companion, but he was able to watch them in the mirror that spanned the wall opposite the counter and gave a view of the entire restaurant.

A waitress paused in front of him, pad at the ready to record his order. "Haven't seen you in here before, handsome," she said, her loud twang as musical as an out-of-tune guitar.

He almost cringed as he imagined her comment bellowing through the restaurant for all to hear and drawing Suzanne's attention. He forced himself to smile. "Just brought my wife into town to do a little shopping," he said, hoping to discourage the woman. "Figured I'd wait for her a while in here."

She nodded. "Sure, honey, whatever."

"Just coffee, please," Hart said. "And a bear claw."

She clunked a heavy mug of coffee down in front of him a moment later, wished him well and walked away, eyeing another target who'd entered and sat at the counter several stools down.

Hart released a sigh of relief and glanced at Suzanne's image in the mirror, hoping his conversation with the waitress hadn't drawn her attention. He hadn't had time to change out of his uniform, but then, he hadn't exactly known he'd be following Suzanne to Tucson and trying to look inconspicuous about it.

He sipped his coffee and took a bite of the sweet roll he'd ordered.

Within minutes he realized he was not the only one watching Suzanne and her friend. At a booth about thirty feet from theirs, another man sat watching the two women.

Hart's first thought was that he was imagining things, but a moment later knew he wasn't. He stared at the man. Was he a federal agent? It seemed logical, but the longer Hart watched him, the more certain he became that that wasn't it at all. The man seemed too polished, too conspicuous, yet at the same time not quite conspicuous enough—for a fed.

There was something familiar about him that nagged at Hart, however, something that left him with an uneasy feeling he couldn't shake. But the more he tried to figure out what it was about the man that bothered him, the more it eluded him and the more certain he became that he knew him, or had at least seen him somewhere.

Hart glanced at Suzanne again. She was picking her fork through a small salad and at the same time seemed deeply interested in whatever her friend was saying.

The waitress refilled his cup without comment and walked away. Hart sighed in relief at her silence and glanced back at the other man. He'd begun absently playing a coin around the fingers of his left hand while continuing to watch Suzanne, controlling the coin with his index finger, then rolling it over the middle, playing it with his ring finger, rolling it to the little finger, then all the way back and repeating the process.

Surprise robbed him of breath. Denial gave it back. Hart stared at the man's hand and the coin he was effortlessly sliding about his fingers. It was an unusual and difficult trick, yet surprisingly Hart had known two people who were accomplished at it: Rick Cassidy and Brenner Trent, one of the corps's former head mechanics. Rick had learned it as a child from his father, a banker who'd kept a rare, specially minted silver dollar in his pocket that he played with during meetings and conversations. He'd called it his lucky charm and he'd given it to Rick on his eighteenth birthday.

Hart had never known Rick to be without it.

That memory made him wonder if the recovery team had found it in the wreckage when they'd retrieved Rick's remains.

Brenner Trent had been so fascinated by the trick that he'd nagged Rick for months to teach it to him. Rick had finally consented one night while they were awaiting flight orders for a mission in Panama.

But both men were dead.

Brenner Trent had been killed in an automobile accident shortly after the company returned from the Jaguar Loop mission. His body had been badly burned, but his wife had identified the remains.

Hart stared into the mirror at the reflection of the man. The coin moved effortlessly over, under and between the fingers of his left hand. He raised a coffee cup to his lips with his right. He looked relaxed, nonchalant, normal, except that he never took his eyes off Suzanne.

His hair was dark brown and a bit curly, ragged ends hugging the tops of his ears and his neck. Dark brows curved over eyes whose color Hart couldn't make out, and it appeared that he hadn't shaved in a day or so, or maybe that was just his look. He was dressed in a black T-shirt and black cloth jacket. His shoulders were broad, his chest wide and he didn't wear a watch.

Hart couldn't shake the feeling that he knew the man from somewhere. The sense of familiarity was too strong, as was the suspicion that whatever was going on with Suzanne, and maybe the investigation concerning himself, this man had something to do with it.

Hart glanced at Suzanne again.

Did she know the man was there? Couldn't she feel him watching her?

An ugly but credible thought flashed into Hart's mind. Maybe the man wasn't watching Suzanne as much as he was watching her back. Which could mean he was also watching Hart. The idea made him uneasy. Could he have been the one in the car Hart had spotted behind him several times on the way to Tucson?

Suddenly Suzanne and her friend rose.

Hart grabbed a newspaper someone had left on the adjacent stool and buried his face in it as they passed behind him on their way to the door.

A second later the other man rose and followed them out.

Hart waited a minute before leaving, not wanting Suzanne to spot him. She and her friend had walked across the parking lot to the right, the man to the left. All were getting into their own cars.

He swore, torn between following Suzanne or the man who'd been watching her. He climbed into the Vette and hurriedly scribbled down the number of the license plate on the man's car.

Suzanne pulled out and the man followed.

Hart started the Vette and shoved it into gear. Not exactly the most inconspicuous vehicle to use to follow someone, but then, he hadn't known he'd be playing private detective when he'd bought it.

A red pickup truck pulled into the lot and stopped in front of Hart as he started to back out.

He slammed on his brakes. Get out of the way, he ordered silently, clenching a hand around the steering wheel as he watched a woman who had to be at least ninety slowly climb from the cab of the truck. The driver waited until she was at the door of the restaurant before he pulled away to park.

Hart finally pulled onto the street.

Suzanne's car was sitting at a stoplight at the corner.

The man was gone.

Half an hour later Hart watched her pull into the driveway beside her bungalow and walk into the house.

What the hell had all that been about? Questions spun through his mind, but he had no answers.

The urge to confront her was almost overwhelming, which was exactly why he decided against giving in to it. Overwhelming was too close to uncontrollable, and he couldn't afford that.

Anyway, he didn't always think straight, or with his head, when he was near Suzanne. He turned his car around and drove to the base.

"Roubechard," he said as he entered the office, "here's a license-plate number. See what you can get on it." He tossed the crumpled piece of paper onto the aide's desk without pausing and strode into his office, slamming the door behind him. He needed to be alone—to think.

His notes and the official reports on the Jaguar Loop mission were still on his desk. He sat down and started to shuffle through them. Images of Suzanne instantly began to play havoc with his concentration.

An hour passed before he realized that of the three pages of notes and five reports he'd gone over, he hadn't retained a thing he'd read.

Hart paced the office, drank cup after cup of coffee strong enough to make most men gag and stared endlessly and sightlessly through the window. He glared hatefully at the telephone every time it rang and wasn't a call from her, and gruffly asked Roubechard a half-dozen times what he'd found out on the license-plate number, which was nothing. Then he paced some more.

Patience had never been one of his virtues.

Chapter 9

"Hart," Suzanne said as she swung open the door. Surprise glistened in her eyes. "I...I'm sorry, I didn't expect you."

"I know, but..." Hart's gaze moved over her from head to toe and back again, assessing and hopefully seducing. Her silk pajamas, the color of rich, red wine, shimmered in the porch light she'd switched on when she'd opened the door. The style was simple and tailored, but on her the outfit was the sexiest thing he'd ever seen.

Hart swore silently. Maybe this wasn't such a good idea. But it was too late now. And he didn't have any others. He held out the chocolate cake he'd stopped and bought at the all-night grocery on his way, having remembered that chocolate was her favorite. "I felt like dessert and didn't want to eat it alone."

Suzanne tried to pull her gaze from his and look

at the bakery box he held out, but she couldn't. She knew she should tell him to go. What had happened between them had been a mistake. Maybe one that had been simmering for a long time and been unavoidable, but still a mistake. They lived in different worlds now. They were different people from what they had been.

That was what she'd been telling herself ever since he'd left her at the open house. When he hadn't called or come by. When she'd wanted to see him so badly she'd scoffed at the need for caution and sneered at her suspicions and doubts. But with him standing before her now, so close it felt as if the warmth of his body was reaching out and caressing her skin, she wanted nothing more than for him to stay.

Not seeing him had allowed her time to think, to convince herself that the feelings he aroused in her were merely physical, and not nearly as strong as she imagined.

Or so she'd thought.

She tore her gaze from his finally and glanced at the pink bakery box he held out.

Tell him to go away, a voice inside her pleaded.

She ignored it.

"Is it chocolate?" she asked instead, a teasing lilt to her tone.

Hart laughed softly. "Is there any other kind of dessert worth having?"

She stepped aside to allow him entry. "Then how can I possibly refuse?"

"I was hoping you couldn't." He walked into the kitchen and set the cake on the table.

Suzanne poured and set two cups of coffee on a

serving tray, along with two slices of cake, and carried it into the living room.

Moonlight flowed in through the glass doors that led to the patio. Its glow softly touched the overstuffed white sofa and matching chair that contrasted dramatically with the colorful Indian-print rug, pillows and various potteries, baskets and paintings.

She set the tray on the coffee table and moved to turn on a lamp.

"Don't," Hart said, ignoring the sofa and taking the chair. He had to move more slowly this time. Be careful. He couldn't afford another blunder.

She paused and looked at him.

"I like the moonlight." It was more conducive to his intentions. Soft surroundings and easy light was relaxing and made you forget about the barriers and guards you might normally keep around your emotions…and the truth, if that was what you were trying to hide.

She settled onto the sofa opposite him and smiled. "Me, too."

Time slipped past quickly as they talked about everything except what had brought them back together.

As midnight neared Hart startled himself by realizing that instead of working the situation, he'd actually been enjoying himself. A string of self-damning curses tripped through his mind. What in hell was the matter with him? His concentration on a situation was normally infallible, yet he was no nearer the truth now than when he'd arrived. He'd become so comfortable he'd nearly fallen into his own trap.

"This was nice tonight," he said, "just sitting

here and talking with you. Relaxing. And I'll tell you, I needed some relaxing after today.''

Suzanne's brows rose slightly. ''Oh? Did you have a bad day?'' She thought of her own. It hadn't exactly been a joy or even fruitful. But that was something she had no intention of sharing with him, because if she told him she'd met with Brenner Trent's widow, she'd have to tell him why, and that meant confessing that she'd taken the personnel files. But then maybe he already knew she'd taken them.

''Bad day? Yeah,'' Hart said. ''You could call it bad. But I'm afraid it's going to be a lot worse tomorrow. I think I'm going to have to put my aide, Marcus Roubechard, on report.''

She felt a start of surprise. ''That nice young man with the tattoo? Why?''

''Some of the background files you and I were going over are missing. I think 'that nice young man' may have given them to the feds.''

She nearly choked on her coffee and couldn't stop herself from glancing at the large purse sitting on the floor near her bedroom door. She hadn't had a chance to put the files back.

''Too bad,'' Hart went on. ''I like him. He's a good kid. Most likely would have made a damned good soldier.'' He watched her closely.

Panic niggled at Suzanne's nerves. ''But why would Private Roubechard take any of those files?''

Hart shrugged. ''Who knows, Suzanne? Some FBI hotshot probably promised him something. Roubechard wants to be career military, follow in his father and grandfather's footsteps and fight for his country. Family tradition and all that garbage, you know? But—'' Hart reached for his coffee ''—he didn't go to college, so he's got a long way to go to become an officer.'' He shrugged. ''My guess is some fed probably made him an offer he felt he couldn't refuse.''

''But…couldn't the files have just been misplaced or something? I mean, why would he…'' She couldn't believe this was happening. They'd been finished with the files. She'd heard Hart tell Roubechard to put them away. How had he discovered any were missing?

Hart shook his head. ''No. They've been boxed and in my office ever since you and I were working on them. And I keep my office door locked when I'm out. Roubechard is the only other person with a key.''

Suzanne damned herself for not putting the files back, but that wasn't going to do any good now. She couldn't let an innocent man take the blame for what she'd done. She summoned every ounce of courage she possessed. ''I took the files, Hart. Not your aide.''

He stared at her, feigning surprise. ''You took them? But why?''

She turned, not wanting to meet his eyes, and stared at one of the paintings that hung on the wall, a scene of a desert landscape, the sun rising above a ragged plateau, a small wagon train moving through the valley below. ''I wanted to look them over for myself.''

''You didn't trust me to tell you the truth?''

She heard the skepticism in his tone and looked back at him. It was apparent immediately that the move had been a mistake. The infinite darkness of

his eyes pulled at her, reminding her of everything
she wanted from him and everything she couldn't
have. "You don't trust me."

A slow smile pulled at the corners of Hart's
mouth. It was fruitless to deny her comment. They
both knew it was all too true. He trusted no one.
Not anymore. "Touché," he said.

She drew herself up, deciding to go on while she
still had some courage left. "I have some concerns
I feel you don't share, Hart. Concerns about some
of Rick's old friends."

"Including me?"

"There are just too many questions without answers." She looked away again, knowing if she continued to meet his gaze, continued to let herself look
into those fathomless midnight-blue eyes, she
wouldn't be able to go on. "I thought if I looked
over the reports myself, maybe some of the questions would be answered."

"Were they?"

She sighed. "No. The reports only stirred up more
questions in my mind."

He remembered which files Roubechard had said
were missing. "So tell me about them," he said.

Long minutes later, after she'd explained what unanswered questions were still bothering her, Hart
pondered her concerns as she walked into the
kitchen and got them more coffee.

His dark gaze caught and imprisoned hers just as
she returned to the sofa, setting his cup on the table
between them.

He leaned forward.

She sat back.

Hart noticed the silent retreat.

"I was the only one to see Rick's chopper shot down, Suzanne, because the squad had split into pairs in order to attack the enemy from several sides. Rick was my partner. We were flying in to attack from the rear. No one else was nearby."

She stiffened. "Which means it might not have happened the way you said."

"It might not have," he said coolly.

A harshness tinged his tone, and a chilling coldness flashed into his eyes. "But it did."

Silence, tense and brittle, hung between them for several seconds before Hart continued.

"Lane Banner left the service after we returned from the mission because he discovered that his wife was seriously ill. He wanted to be with her every minute she had left."

Suzanne was overcome by guilt and compassion. She remembered Lane and his wife, Annie. They'd been devoted to each other.

"Is she all—"

"She died five months ago. She'd been hiding her illness from Lane so he wouldn't jeopardize his career and quit the corps." Hart paused a moment, as if thinking about his next words. "He's returned to duty, but wasn't assigned to the corps, though I know he's requested to be transferred here. If the decision comes down to me," Hart nodded, "he'll get back in."

Suzanne suddenly wasn't so certain of anything, especially her suspicions. "Hart, maybe I—"

"Brenner Trent died in an automobile accident a couple of weeks after our return," he went on, ignoring her interruption. "He fell asleep at the wheel, and his car went off the road and into a ravine."

Suzanne nodded. Trent's widow had almost broken down in the restaurant as she'd described the night she'd gotten the call that her husband had been killed in an automobile accident.

"The chief and his two mechanics are still on duty with the corps and checked out clear. And Zack Morrow and Rand Towler were just rookies at the time of the Jaguar Loop mission. They were included in it only as backup pilots, if that became necessary." He looked at her pointedly. "It didn't."

Suzanne turned and stared at the night beyond the room's sliding glass doors. He'd erased her doubts about everyone but himself.

"I guess that just about eliminates all your suspects, Suzanne, except for me," he added softly as if reading her thoughts.

She looked back at him, into those fathomless blue eyes, and felt a tug at every string dangling from her heart. The last person in the world she wanted to be guilty of murdering Rick, of stealing the plans and trying to frame her for it was Hart.

Anyone but him, her heart cried.

"I went to see Brenner Trent's widow today," she said, deciding she wanted no more lies and half-truths between them. At least, not if she could help it.

Hart's gaze remained locked on hers. So that was who the woman in the restaurant had been. He'd only met Trent's wife once, which explained why she'd seemed somewhat familiar to him, yet he hadn't been able to place her. "Why? Didn't you believe Trent was dead?"

Suzanne smiled at the cutting remark. She deserved it and more, after what she'd done. "No,

I…'' She pulled in a deep breath, knowing she had to start at the beginning if he was going to understand. ''Years ago, while I was attending college, I worked part-time as a clerk at Fort Monmouth, in Virginia.''

''Monmouth.'' He nodded. ''Military Intelligence training center,'' Hart said, his interest piqued.

''Yes. I handled the personnel files of incoming trainees. It was rather tedious work, checking to make certain all proper documents were there, everything that needed to be stamped was stamped, what shouldn't be there wasn't and so on. To make the time pass more quickly I used to play a game with myself.'' She paused, expecting him to comment. When he didn't, she continued, feeling even more foolish and self-conscious. ''I made up personalities for the files. Imagined what the men the files belonged to must be like.''

He wasn't quite sure where she was headed, but he didn't interrupt.

''After I graduated from college I left Monmouth. A few months later I met and married Rick. We moved around a lot, and then we came here. One day he introduced me to Brenner Trent, and I remembered the unusual name and boyish face from a file I'd processed at Monmouth.''

Hart's interest zoomed up. ''Trent went to Monmouth?''

''Yes.''

Why hadn't he known? ''You're sure?''

''Yes.''

Had Lewis known? Had Rick? ''Did Rick know about this?''

She shook her head. ''I don't know. I never mentioned it to him or to Brenner Trent because I knew the information was classified.''

Hart stood and walked to the glass doors. He looked out at the moon-touched horizon without really seeing it, his mind too lost in thought as he remembered the late mechanic, and realized there wasn't much in particular to remember about him. He'd been rather quiet, did his job well, got along with the other guys, and about six months before his death he'd gotten married.

He did remember that Brenner had been crazy about his new wife. Had talked about her incessantly, until some of the guys, including Rick, had started razzing him about being ''obsessed.''

''Anyway,'' Suzanne said, breaking into Hart's thoughts, ''I know Brenner Trent is dead and can't be any more responsible for what's happening now than Rick—'' she shook her head, still puzzled ''—but the fact that an aviation mechanic had been at Monmouth for intelligence training and there's no indication of it at all on his background report has been nagging at me ever since I read the report. I mean, I know they were only preliminary reports, but still...'' She shrugged. ''I'm probably being silly.''

''Did you bring that up with Trent's widow?''

Suzanne shook her head. ''Not really. She was pretty devastated by his death. Still on the verge of tears every time she mentioned his name.''

''So what did you two talk about?''

''I just said I was in town on business, and wanted to convey my condolences, that's all.''

Hart looked back at her. Was this another move in her game plan? He decided to play one of his own. He might be warning her or giving himself away, or he might just learn something from her reaction. He had to risk it. "Have you noticed anyone following you?"

"Following me?" She remembered the sensation she'd felt for days after the FBI had questioned her, as if someone was watching her. Suzanne suddenly realized she hadn't felt it since the first day she'd arrived back in Three Hills. "No, I mean, not since I arrived here." She frowned. "Why?"

Alarm shone from her eyes, and he noticed her hands had begun to tremble in response to his question.

For a brief moment he felt like the proverbial snake in the grass and considered telling her about the man in the restaurant who'd been watching her and Trent's widow. But that would mean admitting that he'd followed her, and that, the voice of reason pointed out, just might be exactly the kind of thing she was after: realization that she'd gotten to him, that a part of him believed her claims.

No, he was too good an officer, too cautious and well trained a soldier to let his guard down completely. He couldn't forget that although a part of him desired her desperately, that was all it was. Desire. As far as he was concerned, there was no such thing as love except in fairy tales. That cold fact of life had been proved to him time and time and again. And trust? He nearly scoffed. Trust was something he would give to no one, especially Suzanne.

"You just need to be careful, Suzanne, that's all," he said. "Don't be going out and questioning people on your own. Exert caution, at least until we find out what's going on."

"Caution." She nodded. Around him, too? "I know it was a dumb idea, but I didn't know what else to do. I mean, that absence about Trent was the only thing in the files that stuck out, you know?" She inhaled deeply. "Hart, I just want this whole mess... I don't want you to be..."

He heard the catch in her voice as it broke over the words and saw the tears that glistened in her eyes, then slipped over her eyelids and, touched by the moon's soft glow as it filtered past him and into the room, turned to shimmering silver trails that coursed down her cheeks.

The need to hold her, to protect her, to love her, rushed through him, stronger than he could deny, more urgent than he could resist. Suddenly he didn't care who was lying and who was telling the truth; he didn't care what had happened a year ago, yesterday or even what tomorrow might bring. All he cared about was now, this moment, and Suzanne.

Settling onto the sofa beside her, he dragged her into his arms. Her breasts crushed against his chest, her body pressed against his. He found it almost impossible to breathe as fires of need licked and flowed through his veins, burned his loins and threatened to rob him of every rational thought he'd ever had.

He could take her now. He could take what he'd always wanted, what he'd always dreamed of. He could use her passion to get at the truth, a little voice in the back of his mind urged.

"Hart," Suzanne whispered, slipping her arms around his neck, catching his gaze with hers.

His lips came down on hers, demanding a response, daring her to refuse him what he craved, what he needed.

His arms tightened their hold on her, melding every svelte line and sensuous curve of her body to every honed length and hard plane of his own. He ravished her mouth, drinking in the sweetness of her kiss and demanding more. She made him forget that for every action, there was always a consequence.

Sanity fled Suzanne's mind. This was what she'd wanted for so long, these feelings that his kisses, his touches, incited within her. This was what she had been seeking, what she had been waiting for all her life: this dangerous man who made her feel things she'd only dreamed about, whose touch or mere presence made her oblivious to everything else in the world, even the danger that with him, because of him, there might not be a tomorrow for her.

She tightened her arms around his neck, wanting never to let go.

Lost in the desires that overwhelmed her, Suzanne was nevertheless more aware of him than she'd ever been. The combined scents of crisp morning air and sultry desert darkness clung to him, a redolence that was uniquely him, while beneath that was the aroma of the man himself, a blend of soap and flesh and passion that was too heady and exhilarating to resist.

She felt his body surround her, his desires meld with her own, the heat of his hands burn into her flesh like branding irons.

Then abruptly his lips left hers.

Suzanne opened her eyes, feeling suddenly more alone and bereft than ever before in her life. Her gaze instantly locked with his.

"I've wanted you since the first moment I saw you," Hart said, his voice husky with emotion.

"I know," she whispered. A delicious shiver of desire coursed through her. "I've wanted you, too." It was a confession she'd never thought she would make, and now she couldn't remember why she'd held it back.

What little sanity and restraint Hart still possessed instantly fled at her words. His lips moved down the slender length of her neck again, across the subtle curve of her shoulders, then made a slow, teasing return trip and recaptured her mouth. His kiss demanded all she had to offer and more, but this time promised to give as much in return.

His hands slipped under her nightshirt, his fingers brushed over, then encircled her bare breasts. She heard his sharp intake of breath and felt a rush of need that shook her to the core of her being.

She clung to him, needing his touch, wanting more, wanting everything he had.

Outside, dark clouds had overtaken the sky, and a deep, growling roll of thunder swept across the desert.

She had wanted him for so long. The loneliness, need and urgency of long-pent-up and denied emotions raged through her, released by the passion of his touch. Her body was on fire, and she was being consumed. It left her languid in his arms and fueled her desire.

Outside a crack of lightning momentarily lit the earth in a blinding flash, announcing the arrival of the first summer storm of the season.

Just as suddenly sanity seized Suzanne and tore

her from Hart's arms. She wanted him desperately, but she couldn't let that happen.

Everything in her screamed at her to trust him, to give herself to him, to love him.

But what if she was wrong?

Damn her. Why wouldn't she listen to him? He pulled a cigarette from his pack, placed it between his lips and flicked open the silver lighter his wife had given him for their twentieth wedding anniversary.

He glanced at the cigarette lighter and ran his thumb over the inscription she'd had engraved on its back. It was too dark now to read it, but he didn't really need to. He knew what it said. "I will love you always, forever, and beyond. D."

It was all he had left.

He flicked the lighting cylinder and a flame burst to life, momentarily illuminating the interior of the car and casting shadows on his face as he drew it into the end of the cigarette.

If they'd been watching they would have seen him then, but he knew they weren't.

The last thing Hart wanted to do was leave her. He looked back at Suzanne, standing on the dark porch. He'd lost it. His resolve. His self-discipline. His control. She'd kissed him, held him, and he'd forgotten everything but his need for her, the lust that tore at his body like a hungry mistress. He was a fool.

He could still feel her lips on his, her body pressed to his length, and wondered if the feeling would ever go away, if he would ever forget.

She could be a traitor, he told himself. A murderer. But the passion he knew he shouldn't be feeling, didn't want to feel, wouldn't cool.

Whatever else he did for the rest of the night, he knew sleep wasn't going to be much a part of it, if at all. Before long and at this rate he'd probably turn into a zombie.

He watched her step from the porch, disappear into the shadows of the house and close the door.

The porch light went out.

Even though he had no proof to the contrary, it was becoming more difficult with the passing of each hour to believe her guilty.

If he'd had half a brain, he would have told Major Lewis about her claims the moment she'd come to him and made them, then refused to have any more to do with her.

He drove through town on his way home. Three Hills was one of the oldest towns in the state and had hosted just about every Old West outlaw, gunslinger and lawman known to history at one time or another. Most of the old buildings had been preserved, and any new ones were designed to fit in.

Usually, whenever he drove through town, he admired the preservation efforts. Tonight his thoughts were too filled with Suzanne to notice anything other than the direction back to his apartment.

If Rick hadn't confided in Suzanne, then how would she have known about the plans for the weapons-detection system? He pulled into his garage. And if she hadn't known about the plans, she couldn't have conspired to steal them.

Unless she'd been involved with someone else in the corps who had that information.

Damn. He climbed out of the car and slammed the door in fury.

He'd held her in his arms, tasted her kiss and almost lost himself to her—and for those few brief moments he'd forgotten that she could have come back to destroy him.

Chapter 10

Suzanne set the laptop computer she'd rented on the coffee table, plugged its phone cord into the wall jack beside the fireplace, then sat cross-legged on the floor and turned it on.

Within seconds she was on the Internet. "Heaven help me," she muttered. She wasn't a computer person, had used one only a few times since she and Clyde had opened the gallery. Clyde, on the other hand, was a computer whiz. He did all their bookkeeping, bill-paying, taxes and whatever else he could on the computer, and was always lauding its attributes and nagging her to learn how to use it and stop writing everything down on notepads.

She hit the search button and typed in "Branson."

The first thing she got for her efforts was a page full of advertisements for Branson, Missouri, which had labeled itself the new home of country music.

After that she found Branson Golf Clubs, Branson Financial Aid, Branson Antique Toys, Branson Foods and Branson Appaloosas.

Hart brought her everything from transplants to Valentine's Day cards, even though it wasn't spelled with an E.

She gave up and called Clyde.

"Suzanne, honey, do you know what time it is? Or did you fly to another time zone?" Clyde squeaked when she said hello and asked him for help.

She glanced at her watch. "Sorry," she mumbled, not having realized it was two in the morning and she'd been zipping from one Web site to another for almost two hours. Though all in vain.

Clyde groaned. "Well, I'm up now, thank you, darling, so what is it you're trying to do?"

Half an hour and a lot of evasive answers to his questions later, she was convinced there was no information on the Web about Hart Branson. But now she knew what she was doing, sort of, and she wasn't through. She thanked Clyde and told him to go back to sleep.

"Oh, yes, right. After this?" he squawked, and promptly hung up.

The moon disappeared and the sun began to rise over the distant horizon. The sky went from black, to gray, to a brilliant blue, and Suzanne slammed the lid of the computer shut and cursed soundly. She was exhausted, and she'd found nothing.

She sat on the sofa, lay her head back and dozed.

Half an hour later the phone rang.

"Suzanne?" It was Clyde.

She nearly groaned aloud. The last thing she wanted to do was answer questions.

"Sorry, love, but I forgot to tell you that someone called for you last night. A man."

She didn't need to see her cousin to know he'd just smiled mischievously and rolled his eyes. "And do you remember who it was?"

"Oh, yes, Agent Smith, or Schmidt, or something like that."

Her heart ceased its beat, and her body turned cold.

"He said he was with the FBI and needed to ask you a few questions. Hah! I mean, really, Suzanne, you should find a man a little more creative than that."

"Did you tell him where I am?" she asked, feeling more than ever like a fugitive.

"Well, not likely," Clyde snipped. "I mean, heavens, I'm not a simpleton, Suzanne. I figured if you wanted him to know, he would know."

She said a prayer of thanks that she'd decided not to tell Clyde what was going on.

"Good. You were right. I'll call you tomorrow."

"I thought you were going to be home tomorrow," Clyde half wailed.

"Soon," she said, and hung up, then dialed her cousin's number. "Please let her have come home," she prayed.

"Molly, it's Suzanne. I need your help," she said the moment her cousin answered. An image of Hart flashed into her mind, and something like pain stabbed at her heart. Tears suddenly stung her eyes, fear burned in her throat and she struggled to talk past both. She didn't want to believe the worst of him and hadn't wanted to involve Molly in this, but she had no choice now—to either one.

Going to Hart for help had been the wrong thing to do. She knew that now. Whatever she felt for him, her traitorous emotions were starting to cloud her judgment, and if that happened, she just might pay for it with her life.

Son of a... DeBraggo threw the receiver he'd been using to listen in on Suzanne's conversations into the glove box of his car and rubbed his ear. He hadn't expected that. Their contact at the State Department was supposed to have seen to it that the cousin couldn't be reached until at least the first of the month, and that was another week away.

He swore again. Someone had screwed up, royally, and now there was going to be a wrench in the works he hadn't anticipated and sure as hell didn't need. Because if it all went wrong, he had no doubt who they were going to blame.

Flipping open his cell phone, he dialed the number of his superior. He got the man's voice-mail. Of course. Mr. Important was never there when he was needed. "Your contact in the State Department screwed up," DeBraggo said, throwing tact and caution to the wind. "The cousin's back and Cassidy contacted her. Everything is going to go to hell if we don't cut her off. Get that damned cousin away from the computer banks and out of town. Now!" he snapped.

He cut the connection. Why was it whenever he stuck his damned neck out there was usually no one there to help, but always someone around to try to chop off his head?

* * *

When Suzanne failed to answer his knock, Hart glanced through the window beside the front door and saw that she was out on the patio. He walked around the house.

Suzanne turned at the sound of his footsteps on the brick walkway.

Hart smiled. It was obvious he'd surprised her.

"I didn't mean to startle you," he said, hoping the apology sounded sincere. He'd never been one to worry about hiding his emotions, except around Suzanne when Rick had been alive. Now he found it more difficult than ever. But he had to succeed. His life might very well depend on his acting ability.

"Sorry," Suzanne said, but her tone was cool, and she didn't return his smile. "I guess I was lost in old memories. I was thinking about Rick, about some of the things he'd said, and—" she shrugged "—I didn't hear the doorbell." In actuality her thoughts had been snapping back and forth between Hart and Molly. She just wished her cousin would hurry up and call back. Maybe then she'd have some answers. She prayed they'd be the right ones.

Hart felt something like jealousy stir in him, hot and unexpected at her comment. Self-loathing instantly followed. How could he be jealous of a dead man? Her husband—his best friend?

He was losing it. Mentally and physically, he was losing it all. He shook the thought aside. No. It was just a battle like none he'd ever fought, and if she was guilty, she was an enemy like none he'd ever faced. "Sorry." He forced the smile to remain on his lips. "I didn't ring the doorbell," he said. "I glanced through the window and saw you sitting back here, so…''

''Oh.''

He watched her set her cup of coffee on a table near the chaise longue and knew she was more shaken by his unannounced visit than he'd originally thought. But why? Because he'd come by? Or had something gone wrong with her plan?

Her phone rang. ''Excuse me,'' Suzanne said, walking inside to answer it.

Hart punched a fist into his other hand. Normally he loved the cat-and-mouse game of battle. But not this time. With Suzanne he hated it, and that had made him careless. He should have gotten her talking about Rick when she'd brought him up. Now it was too late.

''That was my business partner,'' Suzanne said, stepping back outside. ''He had some questions about an upcoming assignment.''

Hart watched her walk toward him, watched how her lips moved as they formed each word, watched her fold her arms together. He remembered what it had felt like when he'd held her to him, pressed her body into his and captured her mouth with his. An ecstasy he might never know again and shouldn't have known in the first place—at least not with Suzanne Cassidy.

''Did you ask him about DeBraggo?'' Hart said. ''How the man might have known where you were staying when you were at the hotel?''

''Oh, no, I didn't have to.'' She shook her head. ''I guess I forgot to tell you, Mr. DeBraggo explained. He fibbed about talking to Clyde, but was reluctant to approach me without claiming some prior contact with the gallery. He'd seen my picture with an article the *New York Times* did on a purchase I made on behalf of the gallery a few weeks ago.'' She shrugged. ''It was just coincidence we were both in the same hotel, but...''

''Yeah,'' Hart said, not believing it for one minute. ''Coincidence.'' He could count on one finger the number of times he'd believed an incident was a coincidence, and there was still a lot of doubt in his mind on that one.

Suzanne heard the derision in his tone and frowned. ''You don't believe that?'' His skepticism made her nervous and, in spite of herself, afraid.

''Let's just say I've never encountered a coincidence I liked,'' Hart drawled.

His comment stirred doubts and unnerved her further. What if he was right and Mr. DeBraggo wasn't who he'd claimed? Then who was he?

Hart watched the fear shadow her eyes and realized he'd upset her, which was what he should have avoided. ''Hey, ignore me,'' he said, and laughed. ''I've never been known as much of an optimist, so what do I know? I'd probably be suspicious of the Pope.''

She laughed, but he didn't miss the uneasiness that edged the sound.

''I mean, he's probably exactly what he says,'' he added.

Suzanne nodded, feeling a bit relieved and knowing she probably shouldn't be. ''Was there any special reason you came by this morning?'' she asked when silence fell over them. ''Have you found out something?''

''I was hoping we could have breakfast together,''

he said. "Maybe at that new little café they built down by the old jail." God help him, in spite of everything, his desire for her, his need for her, was stronger than ever.

She wanted desperately to say yes, but knew she couldn't, so she shook her head. "I don't think so, Hart. I have a lot of phone calls to make this morning for gallery business, and I don't feel well at all today," she added quickly, to ward off an invitation to lunch or dinner. She touched her stomach to add credence to her words. "Maybe something I ate last night. But thank you for asking." She had to stay away from him, keep some distance between them until Molly called back. It was the only way she could think of to keep her emotions under control, and herself safe.

Ever since she'd nearly let him make love to her, she'd been unable to think of anything else for more than a few minutes at a time, and that was when they were apart. When he was near, her thoughts of him raided her senses and banished every other subject from her mind as if no other existed.

Hart leaned against the door of his Cobra and watched the rookie who had joined the corps a month ago take a training chopper through a series of difficult, though basic, maneuvers.

But Hart's thoughts weren't on the rookie or the exercise. They were on Suzanne, on accusations he still found difficult to believe, an investigation into his own background he could find no justification for and an invitation to breakfast she had turned down. He hadn't expected her to say no.

His cell phone rang.

He answered, expecting to hear Suzanne before remembering she didn't have the number.

"Senator Trowtin on the line for you, sir," Roubechard said.

The line clicked twice as Roubechard transferred the call.

Hart tensed.

"Captain," the senator said, "I'm calling you from a secure phone, and I hope to hell that aide of yours can be trusted to forget he even received this call."

"He can, sir," Hart said, hoping it was the truth.

Then he's not a suspect. Suzanne's words flashed through Hart's mind.

"You'd better be right, Captain." The senator's tone was gruff and hurried. "I've got something for you that might help, but you didn't hear it from me, is that agreed?"

"Yes, sir."

"Good. Get your hands on a copy of Lieutenant Richard Cassidy's autopsy report as soon as you can. Then get yourself a copy of the records the retrieval crew wrote up on what was left of his chopper when they finally located it."

"Is there—?"

"I don't have time to answer questions, Captain. Get those records, and you'll find some of the answers you need. Then take a long, hard look at your corps members again. And I mean, look long and hard. My info says you've got at least one man in the group who shouldn't be there. He lied about his past when he joined up. Was in the state pen for five years on an assault-and-battery. And if you don't already know it, there's a Federal agent watching you and the Cassidy woman."

"Who?"

"His name's Sal Buenotarres, but he sometimes uses the cover name Salvatore DeBraggo."

"DeBraggo," Hart echoed, surprised. He'd been fairly certain the Spaniard was not what he'd appeared to be, but he would have tagged him as one of the bad guys.

"That's it, Captain," the senator said, breaking into Hart's thoughts. "If I get anything else of substance, I'll get it to you, one way or another. But don't call me if it's not a matter of life or death."

The line went dead.

Hart stared at the training chopper, circling in the distance, as the senator's last words repeated through his mind.

"He's pretty good for a rookie," Zack said, saluting Hart.

Hart turned. He stared at the other man, momentarily disoriented. How long had he been standing there? How much had he heard?

Zack frowned. "You okay, Captain?"

Hart shook himself mentally. He had to get a grip. "Yeah, I'm, fine." He glanced back at the rookie, his chopper now hovering over the runway a few hundred yards away, then looked back at Lieutenant Zack Morrow. Silver-lensed, aviator-style dark glasses hid Zack's eyes from view, while a black Stetson shaded his face, both complementing his flight suit.

"So, when are we going to take the newbie out to the Gulch?" Zack said, a devilish grin pulling at his handsome features.

Hart shrugged. "You want to take him out tomorrow?" he asked, knowing Zack would say yes.

The Gulch was one of the final tests for a recruit transferring into the Cobra Corps, and Hart knew that Zack loved flying it and putting a rookie through his paces almost as much as he'd once loved riding on the back of an angry bull.

"Sure thing, boss, but aren't you coming?"

Hart always went on the Gulch runs.

He tucked the clipboard under his arm. "Not this time. I've got a few other things to take care of." Like saving his career—and finding out if the woman he couldn't stop thinking about and who had turned his passion into his enemy was a murderous traitor. "Radio him in, would you, Zack? I've got to go."

The sun was just settling beyond the horizon, the air starting to cool, as Hart returned to his office. Roubechard greeted him with more bad news. "I've, um, been listening to the tape of Ms. Cassidy's phone calls, sir, like you ordered, and..."

Listening to the tapes—or doctoring them? The suspicion flashed into Hart's mind, instant and unbidden. He just as instantly chastised himself for it. Roubechard was not a suspect.

"And, well, sir, I think, uh..."

"Oh, hell, spit it out, Roubechard," Hart said curtly, the normally tightly held rein on his patience long gone.

"Yes, sir, well, sir, uh, Ms. Cassidy placed another call to France."

Terrific. No, more than terrific, Hart thought, feeling a real urge to put his fist through the wall. Absolutely wonderful.

"I thought you'd want to listen for yourself, sir." Roubechard switched on the tape.

"*Oui*, Marsei residence."

Hart felt all his hopes plunge, his dreams die and every dark suspicion and flame of anger in him flare beyond his control.

After the initial pleasantries were exchanged, Robert Marsei asked if everything was finalized.

"No," Suzanne said. "We've run into a few complications."

"Can you handle them?"

"Yes, we're working on them. It shouldn't be much longer. I think Clyde is planning to make the final delivery himself."

"Good," Robert said. "Good. It has been too long since I've seen him. Well, *mon amie,* it has been a pleasure doing business with you, as usual."

The blackness of Hart's mood deepened. She was doing business "as usual" with Robert Marsei. Could there be any real doubt she was guilty? Everything in him screamed no, yet deep inside a part of him still wanted to say yes and believe in her.

But that wasn't the cold, logical side he counted on for survival, and it wasn't a part of himself he could afford to listen to.

He'd known better than to let his emotions get out of control. Too much was at stake. And like a fool, he'd allowed it to happen, anyway.

Whether he'd just fallen into her trap or dug a hole of his own didn't matter. He was no closer to the truth of this whole mess than he'd been when it had started, and he was a helluva lot less objective.

"Lock it in my safe," he said as Roubechard turned the tape off.

"Yes, sir, but there's something else, sir."

"What?" he snapped, no longer concerned with protocol, manners or even the other's man's feel-

ings. He needed "something else" like he needed a
damned bullet between the eyes.

"Ms. Cassidy called someone in the State Department and asked them to do background checks
on all the corps members. Including you, sir."

"Son of a…" He didn't need this. Hart's temper
ripped from his control. He stood abruptly, his chair
scraping the floor and nearly toppling.

Roubechard stepped back hurriedly, a look of surprise on his face as Hart stalked past him to the door.
"Sir?"

Hart spun. "What, Roubechard? Don't tell me
you've got more good news."

"Uh, no, sir. I just wanted to know if you're
checking out for the day, sir."

"Yes, I'm out," he said. "So don't call me unless
our enemies are on their way and the damned world
is about to explode."

"Yes, sir," Roubechard said, snapping to attention and saluting.

Hart stalked out, slamming the door behind him.
Then he stopped, remembering that Roubechard
took everything he said quite literally. Swearing, he
walked back into the office. "I didn't mean that,
Roubechard. Call me if you come up with anything
else." He grabbed a cell phone and slipped it into
his pocket.

"Anything, sir?"

"Yes, Roubechard, anything." There was no telling anymore what might or might not be important.
He held up the cell phone and said, "Number five,"
then walked to his car and slid in behind the wheel.

Damn it all. He didn't have any more time to
spare. If Suzanne was guilty, and that *if* was looking

more and more probable, then she was trying to find another way to lay the blame for treason, and murder, at his doorstep. But on the thinning chance that she was innocent, a State Department geek poking his nose into the military's top-secret business could escalate the danger to both her and him, if the wrong people found out.

In his experience with the feds, the wrong people usually always found out. And that usually ended up with a stockpile of dead bodies.

He jammed the car into gear and spun away from the building. Adding his body to the stockpile was not in his game plan. In battle maybe, but not this way.

Anger seared through his veins, and though he was loath to acknowledge it, fear seized his heart. He didn't know what to feel and what to damn, but he knew he was tired of tiptoeing around his suspicions.

He'd let himself go too far with her and was probably lucky he was even still alive.

Chapter 11

Suzanne heard the squeal of tires on pavement, then the crunch of gravel as tires spun over the driveway of her rented bungalow.

A car door slammed.

Fear instantly pulled her into its dark grasp and she tensed. Had the FBI finally come for her? She stared at the door, expecting to hear the bell.

Instead, a fist crashed against the door.

Suzanne jumped, startled.

"Suzanne?"

Hart, not the FBI. Relief and joy swept through her, momentarily pushing all thoughts of caution aside. She ran to the door and flung it open, heedless of the fact that all she had on was a sheer batiste nightgown.

"Why the hell was Carger here?" Hart demanded as he stormed past her into the living room. He spun around to face her, confront her, and his breath instantly stalled in his throat. She stood in the moonlit doorway, her body silhouetted by the night's soft light filtering in behind her. The sheer nightgown she wore was like a veil of transparent cloud, accentuating every inch of her and concealing nothing from his sight. Desire flared to life within him, but he fought it off. This was not the right time and she was not the right woman. He swallowed, hard. "Why was the chief here, Suzanne?" he repeated, his voice gruff now with the unwanted emotions flowing through him. "And what the hell kind of business are you doing with Robert Marsei?"

She stared at him, startled. "I...the chief was... Robert is..."

His anger left him no patience. "Who did you call in the State Department, Suzanne? I had the personnel reports—you could have asked me for them, looked at them with me anytime you'd wanted. Instead, you stole them. And now you've called in the State Department? What are you trying to do, Suzanne? Destroy me?"

Her jaw fell. "Destroy you?"

"Dammit," Hart cursed. Maybe without that halo of light around her she wouldn't look so damned tempting. He stalked past her and kicked the front door closed.

It slammed against its frame with a deafening thud.

Suzanne suddenly realized just how little she had on and grabbed the robe she'd discarded and left lying on the sofa earlier. She struggled into it. "Hart, I..." She'd never seen him like this, and it frightened her.

He grabbed her upper arms and dragged her to

him. "Answer me, Suzanne, dammit. What is Chief Carger to you?"

"Nothing," she said, struggling against his hold on her. But it was no use—his grip was like a vise of iron. "I don't even like Chief Carger. I've never liked him. He tried to warn me away from you when I got back. Said you were called away a lot because of your clearance. That you weren't the kind of man a woman like me should get involved with."

Hart's gaze bored into hers as he searched for any sign she was lying. "Why would he say that to you? Why would he care?"

She shook her head and shrugged. "He said I deserved better."

"And Marsei?"

"Robert?"

"Yes, Robert."

She shook her head, as if confused. "He's a client, Hart, that's all."

He released her so suddenly she nearly lost her balance.

"He's a damned spy, Suzanne." Hart stalked across the room, then spun to glare at her. "Marsei buys and sells government secrets like most people buy and sell their worthless pieces of garbage at flea markets. To the highest bidder."

Suzanne stared at him. This wasn't happening. He couldn't be telling her the truth. She shook her head in denial. "No. That can't be right. Hart, you must have him confused with someone else. Really. Robert is an old friend of Clyde's family. His father grew up and went to school with Robert Marsei."

"Really? Then maybe you'd better look into the activities of Clyde's father, Suzanne, before you take on his friends as customers. I am not mistaking Robert Marsei for someone else. The man is a spy, and one of the best and deadliest in the business. He deals in espionage, Suzanne, and he doesn't care who or what side he works for, who gets hurt or who ends up dead as long as he gets paid.''

''Robert?'' she said again, stunned by Hart's words and unable to reconcile them to the gentle, sophisticated man she knew.

''Who did you call at the State Department?'' Hart demanded again.

She stared at him, her mind still reeling in disbelief at the accusation that Robert was a spy.

''Suzanne!'' Hart snapped, cold fury edging his tone. ''Who did you call at the State Department?''

''My cousin.'' The words were out before she could stop them.

''Why?''

Her gaze became lost in his. Everything in her warned her to stay silent, to send him away, to heed caution. ''To check up on you,'' she said, instead.

His jaw tightened. Fire leaped into his eyes. Anger drew his mouth taut. He clenched his hands into fists.

Suzanne suddenly ached to reach out to him— yearned to run to him.

''Did you kill Rick, Suzanne?''

Her jaw dropped open again, the words, the accusation, like a slap on her face. ''What?'' she finally managed weakly.

''You heard me.'' His tone was cold, hard, calm. ''Did you arrange for Rick's death, then have someone steal the plans and sabotage his chopper?''

''Oh, my God.'' Any fight left in her fled. She

sank to the sofa, her legs trembling so violently they were no longer able to support her. She felt a series of shivers course through her body, one after another, chilling her blood, threatening to stop her heart. "No." She shook her head. "You can't mean someone…that Rick was…"

"That's exactly what I mean," Hart snapped.

Tears filled her eyes. She looked up at him. "No. He can't have been murdered." She shook her head again in denial of the possibility. "No." Her tears spilled over and ran down her cheeks, streams of moisture that turned to trails of silver that glistened in the moonlight filtering in through the patio doors.

In that moment as Hart looked down at her, something happened. He couldn't explain it, didn't understand it, but suddenly all his doubts and suspicions fled. It was unreasonable. Nevertheless it was how he felt. He crossed the room and pulled her into his arms.

"Hart, why did they have to—"

His lips captured hers, stopping her words. His tongue plunged into her mouth, and what little sanity Suzanne had left vanished.

It was exactly what she needed.

"Hart," Suzanne whispered, slipping her arms around his neck, instantly forgetting his anger, his accusations, and feeling nothing but safe in his arms.

His name on her lips was Hart's undoing, like a caress of seduction, whispering to him, stoking the fires of his desire and banishing all doubt and reason from his thoughts. Only one thing remained in his mind—that he had to have her, love her, meld her passion with his own.

The heat of his body enveloped her. He had

kissed her before, but never with such demand, such savage virility, that it robbed the breath from her lungs and the strength from her body.

She clung to him, longing burning within her, need gripping her within a delirium of desire. Whatever else happened in her life, good or bad, she knew that being here now in Hart's arms and loving him was right. He was what she wanted.

His arms around her were suddenly the only reason she remained standing, the pounding of his heart against her breast a cadence that matched the beat of her own.

Her tongue dueled instinctively, wantonly, with his, and a moan of pleasure was torn from Hart's throat, the sound deepening the passion building within Suzanne.

How could she have ever denied what she felt for him, had felt since the moment they'd first met?

Her arms tightened around his neck, her fingers entwined in the golden hair at his nape. Fire erupted in her veins, longing moved through her breasts, and an aching hunger burned deep inside of her.

This was meant to be. Whatever else happened to her, she knew this moment, this feeling, this love and need for him, was meant to be.

"I want you, Suzanne," Hart breathed against her lips, his voice ragged and husky with need.

"Yes," she whispered.

His lips burned through her skin, touching her very soul as they moved down the line of her neck, over the curve of her shoulders, then returned to capture her lips again.

His hand moved to cup her breast, his fingers kneading the tight flesh, his thumb flicking gently over the pebbled nipple, stoking her hunger, heightening her pleasure until she arched against him, aching to be touched everywhere by him, needing him as much as he needed her.

She had never felt such fire.

His lips never left hers as he slid the robe from her shoulders and let it fall to the floor, a soft, billowing cloud of fabric that settled around her ankles. One by one, Hart released the thin silk ribbons that held the front of her gown closed, and then it, too, fluttered silently to the floor.

Hart sank to his knees and pulled her with him, then pushed her gently down so that she lay on the carpet. He knelt over her; his gaze swept her face, over the length of her body, then returned to meet her eyes.

She had never lain naked to a man's assessing gaze before, not even Rick's, and a blush swept over her from head to foot.

"You're more beautiful than all my dreams," Hart said softly.

She knew he meant every word. Her embarrassment instantly disappeared, and she met his gaze boldly. As if all the darkness of his soul, all the pain and hurt, the loneliness and yearning, the joys and dreams of Hart Branson were reaching out to her, she suddenly knew the depth of what it was she'd been feeling for him since that first moment they'd met. And she knew it would never release her. No matter what happened between them now or in a thousand tomorrows to come, it would never let her go.

His lips reclaimed hers, moved down her throat,

then pressed against the sensitive flesh between her breasts.

Suzanne moaned as a wave of pleasure gripped her.

Hot currents of gnawing, demanding need ripped through Hart, but as his hands moved to caress her body, she pulled away from him.

Everything in Hart silently screamed a denial of the desertion.

Suzanne pushed herself to a sitting position and smiled. "My turn now, Captain."

Surprise and pleasure rippled through him.

With a teasing light in her eyes she began to slowly free each button on his shirt, then released the buckle of his belt, the catch on his slacks.

Her hands moved beneath his shirt and pushed it ever so slowly from his shoulders. Hart felt an ache of desire seize him, like a burning rope, cutting off his air, squeezing his body and scorching his loins.

It was almost more than he could stand.

She caressed the ropy length of his arms as she urged the shirt over them and away.

He reached for her, needing to feel her in his arms again, but she smiled and pushed at his chest, holding him off. "Not yet," she said softly.

He dragged a deep breath of air into his lungs to calm the need raging almost out of control inside him.

Suzanne stood, then held out her hands to him and silently urged him to do the same.

She pressed her lips to his chest, feeling the soft, golden hairs that curled there tickle her cheeks. "Mmm, delicious." Her fingers slowly slid the zipper of his slacks down, then urged them and his briefs, inch by teasingly slow and agonizing inch, from his hips.

A jolt of physical need pierced him. Hart nearly groaned at the touch of her hands on his bare legs, at the feel of his jutting arousal brushing lightly against one of her breasts as she bent to free him of his pants, then urged him to kick off his shoes.

The need to drag her into his arms and wrap himself around her, to push himself into her, was a torment he knew he would gladly suffer, if it meant she would always be at its end.

Suzanne stepped back, keeping him at arm's length, and stared at him, a slight smile pulling at her lips.

Moonlight touched his body, turning the sun-kissed golden hue of his skin to burnished bronze, dark shadow edging each muscle and curve, intensifying the aura of strength and steely hardness. Caesar would have put him in charge of his army, she thought. Cleopatra would have taken him to her bed. And Aphrodite would have stolen him into the heavens.

"Like what you see?" Hart said, unable to help himself. His voice was rough with desire and harsh from the self-restraint he was imposing on himself. But it was a question of need, rather than conceit.

His words cut into her fantasies and played with them tauntingly. "Well..." She cocked her head and her gaze raked him, as if assessing every inch for a response to his question.

His body was a long length of solid muscle, and hard with anticipation and the need to be satisfied. He had shoulders that reminded her of mountain ranges, broad and rippled, while his arms were well-honed cords of sinew. A light matting of silky, blond hair covered his chest, thinning and darkening as they came together in a V just above his stomach, then plunged downward and thickened again at the juncture of his thighs.

There was no denying he wanted her, yet even as her gaze was unabashedly drawn to his arousal, she felt an involuntarily shiver of nervousness at the evidence of it jutting so fiercely toward her.

Hart smiled. "I think you've seen enough," he growled, unable to resist pulling her into his arms any longer. His mouth trapped hers, effectively cutting off any protest she might have uttered.

But protest was as far from Suzanne's mind as anything, other than Hart Branson. Her senses spun wildly out of control at his assault. She writhed against him, lost in the euphoria of being in his arms. Her composure was gone, shattered into a thousand splinters as the longing he aroused within her continued to build and deepen, and consume her.

Everything about him was dark and dangerous, even deadly. Everything about him was what she'd sworn never to want again. But it didn't matter anymore. She could no longer deny that he was exactly what she did want. Forbidden or not, she wanted him. Desperately, wholly and forever.

The feather-light exploration of his hands on her body set off flames of need wherever they touched. His thumb rhythmically stroked her nipple, teasing, then deserting it to move slowly, tauntingly, tormentingly downward, gliding seductively past her waist and over her hip.

Reality slipped away as she gave herself up to the world of his kisses and caresses, a world she had tried so desperately not to want. Now the only thought left her, the only desire, was to be possessed by him.

"You're so beautiful," he said, his voice heavy with the emotion that had conquered him. The world had disappeared, and Hart couldn't have cared less. Holding her tightly to him, he lowered them both to the lushly carpeted floor, and while his lips sensuously explored her mouth once again, his hands began a slow, hungry exploration of her body.

Joy filled Suzanne's heart and brought tears to her eyes. She wrapped a leg around one of his, needing him closer. Never in her life had she desired a man so completely.

Each caress was an intoxicating sensation. When his hand slipped between her thighs, a jolt of raw desire swept through Suzanne that threatened to rob her of every shred of sanity she possessed. She cried out his name, and his mouth covered hers, swallowing the sound. His fingers were like fire against her flesh, increasing the gnawing ache of anticipation that had invaded her blood.

His lips moved over her face, her neck, her breasts, kissing her and whispering her name, as if, even as he made love to her, he couldn't believe it was really her, that it was really, finally happening.

Until this moment Hart hadn't realized the depth of loneliness into which his soul had fallen, how intense the darkness in which he existed had become.

But with her there was sunlight again. And hope. If only for a little while.

His body trembled with the force of the emotions her touch unleashed, and he moved to cover her

body with his, to take, to share at last what he'd
never hoped to have. If he'd had any doubts that
Suzanne was capable of arousing feelings and needs
in him like nothing he'd ever felt before, like no
other woman had ever stirred within him, they were
gone now.

Suzanne felt him fill her, then slowly begin to
move inside her, and she wrapped her arms around
him and began to move with him in the ancient,
euphoric rhythm of love.

Suzanne exulted in his possession of her, each
caress of his hands, the hot fusing of their bodies,
melding, loving, becoming one. The soft, silky hairs
on his chest brushed her breasts and teased her nip-
ples.

She looked up and into the dark-blue depths of
his eyes and, for a brief moment, saw all the pain
and loneliness he had endured, the love he had always craved and the love he had to give. The sight
filled her heart.

A moan escaped her lips as pleasure surged
through her and became so intense, so mind-
numbing that all she could do was surrender herself
to it. Nothing in life had prepared her for the intensity of feeling his lovemaking aroused within her.
Heat rushed through her, overtaking every muscle.
Fulfillment replaced need, ecstasy replaced hunger.
She cried out his name, over and over, never wanting him to leave her, never wanting this feeling to
end.

For the briefest of moments her soul touched his,
and Suzanne knew nothing in life would ever be the
same for her again unless he was with her.

Pleasure beyond comprehension seized Hart,

gripped his body, paused the beat of his heart and wiped his mind clear of every thought but of Suzanne. In that moment Hart suddenly knew he was as close as he'd ever been to wanting from her what he'd been afraid of wanting from anyone all of his life.

He wanted to love her and wanted her to love him. He wanted to spend an eternity of days with her and lie with her beside him in his bed every night. He wanted to know she would be there when he came home, would always be waiting for him when he left on a mission, that her arms would welcome him home and her love would warm his soul forever and keep the cold, cruel darkness away.

He held her tightly to him, whispering her name like a chant of love.

Tears of joy and fear, pleasure and anxiety, filled her eyes.

As the rapture of their lovemaking faded to a warm glow, they lay on the floor, entwined in each other's arms, and slept. Moonlight bathed their bodies, turned planes to gold, and curves to midnight shadows.

Suzanne woke, momentarily disoriented, then sighed in contentment and relaxed against Hart. She stared past the glass doors at the night, her gaze drinking in the star-strewn sky, the sliver of moon, the black ragged silhouette of the mountains in the distance.

Unanswered questions filled her mind, unbidden and unwelcome. She wanted the euphoria of their lovemaking to last forever. Instead, she found herself starting to struggle against the doubts and suspicions that were slowly creeping back into her mind.

What if his outrage earlier had been nothing more than an act? His indignation a ruse to lure her further into his trap? His lovemaking the lock that would keep her there?

He had made love to her, made her feel complete and alive in ways she'd never imagined she could feel, yet her fears and loneliness seemed almost intensified, and there was a part of her, a part she wished didn't exist, that still suspected him of murder and betrayal.

A tear slipped from the corner of her eye, followed by another and another, and she suddenly wished she could fall asleep in his arms and never wake up.

Hart felt the moisture of her tears on his chest and wondered at them, but he didn't move. He was still struggling with wonder at the depth of passion and feeling she'd incited in him.

He drew in a long, deep breath and closed his eyes. Every emotion imaginable had burst to life within him while he'd made love to her.

When this thing was over, she would be gone from his life again. He had no doubt of that. Innocence would take her back to her life in California; guilt would take her to prison forever. Either way, all the old feelings of loneliness, anger and resentment would return to him twofold. It was inevitable, but this time he wasn't sure that he had the strength or will to survive living like that again.

A few minutes later he noticed that her tears had stopped, her breathing had quieted, and he knew she'd fallen asleep. He slipped his arm from beneath her and, pushing to his feet, walked to the window and looked out. How in hell had his life turned into such a mess?

Maybe there was no way out of this espionage thing. Maybe his career was already over. He glanced back at Suzanne. Two hours ago he'd drawn her into his arms and said to hell with the world, his suspicions, his doubts and everything else. But now the real world and all its cold, ugly realities and possibilities was back, along with his suspicions and doubts, and though he hated himself for them, he couldn't rid himself of them. At least not until he had proof of the truth.

Gut feeling just wasn't enough anymore.

He turned and stared out at the moon-touched night. What had just happened between them shouldn't have, and it was all his fault. The feelings between them were physical, and if there were any others, they were based on fear, need and maybe nothing more than lies or memories. Guilt hammered at him.

Hart stretched his arms wide, then rolled his shoulders and stretched again.

He heard Suzanne stir and glanced back at her. Her dark hair was splayed out on the rug, and moonlight touched her skin, caressing it with warmth and light. Desire surged anew through him, as hot and fierce as if he'd never touched her. Hart steeled himself against the temptation to lie back down beside her, pull her into his arms again, make love to her again.

How well did he really know Suzanne Cassidy? Maybe as well as he needed. Maybe not at all.

He'd come here to batter down her defenses. Instead, it had been his defenses that had crumbled. Cursing himself for a fool and Suzanne for making him want her to the point of throwing caution to the wind, he turned back to the window. His moment of weakness could end up getting him killed. Maybe getting them both killed, if she truly was innocent.

Or it could just leave him tormented for the rest of his life, if she was guilty.

Grabbing his clothes, he hurriedly pulled them on. He had to go. Now. His gaze moved over her again as he pulled on his boots, everything in him appreciating the curve of her hip, the svelte line of her legs...

Go now, he reminded himself, before the urge to make love to her again became too strong to resist.

DeBraggo drew his jacket more tightly around his chest, crossed his arms over it, tucked his hands into his armpits in an attempt to keep them warm and tried to bury his chin deeper in his open collar. What remained of his coffee had long ago gotten cold, his stomach was growling because he was hungry as hell, and no one had told him that the desert, which was so friggin' hot during the day, could be so bone-chilling cold at night.

He glanced at the bungalow. They were together in there, Captain Branson and Suzanne Cassidy, and they were most likely sound asleep. DeBraggo's gaze swept over the quiet neighborhood, shrouded in darkness. Except for a few stray dogs and prowling cats, no one else was around, and he hadn't seen anyone else watching them.

But if someone wanted Hart Branson and Suzanne Cassidy dead, this was probably the perfect time to do it—unless it was supposed to look like an accident.

The .38 revolver tucked into DeBraggo's shoulder holster pushed into his rib cage as he shifted position on the car seat. Someone else might have found that hard bulge in his side uncomfortable. DeBraggo found it snugly comforting, knowing the piece was there, loaded, ready and deadly, if he needed it.

He sighed. How long had it been since he'd slept in a nice, comfortable, warm bed?

Since he got put on this case, he answered himself, cursing his bad luck.

The deep roar of a car engine broke into the night's silence.

Startled, DeBraggo bolted upright in his seat, banging his elbow on the doorknob and swearing at the teeth-rattling pain that shot through his arm.

The headlights on Hart's Corvette suddenly flared, cutting through the darkness and lighting the street.

Branson was leaving? DeBraggo glanced at his watch. At five in the morning? His thoughts spun as he tried to decide what to do. Why would Branson leave now—unless he'd been wrong and they'd argued?

The minute the Vette was out of sight DeBraggo pulled his car up to the bungalow and ran to the window. If she was all right he didn't want to disturb her, but if she wasn't...

He saw her lying on the living room floor. His heart loped. The SOB had killed her.

The thought no sooner flashed through DeBraggo's mind than Suzanne stirred.

DeBraggo nearly sagged to the ground with relief,

then spun around. She was okay, but where the hell had Branson gone? Sal's info said the man wasn't on duty today.

He ran to his car.

Hart drove as if the hounds of hell were on his tail and only speed would keep them at bay. Anger hammered at his every thought, called him a fool and fed his fears.

It was becoming too hard to believe she was guilty, to even give more than a moment's credence to the dark suspicions and doubts.

He'd seen innocence in her eyes, heard it in her voice, felt it while in her arms. Wouldn't he have been able to tell, while making love to her, if it had all been nothing but a lie?

Or was she that good an actress?

He took a curve in the road without slowing. The car's tires squealed and gobbled up the white line and half of the opposing lane before returning to its own.

Hart glanced in the rearview mirror.

Headlights shone on the road behind him.

If it was the feds, they could eat his dust. He pressed down harder on the accelerator.

Another curve. The headlights behind him disappeared. Hart watched and waited for them to show up in his rearview mirror again, but the road behind him remained dark.

He pulled the Vette into the garage of his apartment. Even if she was innocent—his heart screamed that she was—there was no future for them together. No happily ever after. She had her life in L.A. now. He had his with the army.

Realizing where his thoughts had gone, Hart nearly scoffed aloud, disgusted with himself. What in blazes was he thinking? That they'd be together forever? That Suzanne loved him? That he loved her?

He felt the familiar aloneness of his life suddenly envelop him, like a suffocating mantle, momentarily robbing him of even the will to live. He would remember this night, the hours spent in her arms making love to her, for the rest of his life. It would haunt him when he ached to hold her again, yearned to taste her kisses and feel her body pressed to his.

But all he would have, instead, was the loneliness of longing.

Shaking off his dark thoughts, Hart decided to take a quick shower and get to the base. If Roubechard or Lewis hadn't managed to get a copy of Rick's autopsy report yet, then Hart would call the senator back.

Don't call me unless it's a matter of life or death. The senator's words echoed through his mind.

Well, as far as he was concerned, this was a matter of life or death—his.

Chapter 12

Suzanne felt the bright rays of the morning sun streaming in through the patio doors kiss her skin. She stirred and reached out for Hart.

Her hands found nothing but emptiness.

She opened her eyes, expecting to see him lying just out of her reach, and found she was alone.

Her body tingled at the memory of their lovemaking, then began to ache with the need of his touch. She ran a hand over the empty space of rug beside her and remembered him lying there, holding her, kissing her, loving her.

"Hart?" The sound of her voice hung on the still air of the small house.

He didn't answer.

He'd left. She felt a sense of desertion. He'd left without even saying goodbye. She sat up and looked around, making certain he was actually gone from the bungalow and not just from her side.

Silence filled the air.

She drew her knees up, hugged them to her and remembered the way his hands had moved over her body, caresses that were so gentle, so tantalizing, so teasing, they'd drawn a passion from her deeper than anything she'd ever felt. His lips seemed still imprinted on her own.

It wasn't until after she'd showered and dressed that she glanced at the phone and noticed its message light blinking. She smiled. He'd called. She pressed the playback button.

Molly—not Hart's—voice filled the silence.

"Suz, it's me, Molly. I need to talk to you, but I can't right now. I'll try to call you again later, but for God's sake, whatever you do in the meantime, *keep your nose out of things.*"

The line went dead.

Suzanne stared at the machine, her heart racing almost as fast as the tape she heard rewinding. Keep her nose out of things? That sounded like a warning. Molly had sounded frightened. As if she were making the call while afraid someone was listening or coming after her.

The thought scared Suzanne half to death. She picked up the phone and hurriedly dialed her cousin's home number. The phone rang, one, two, three, four, five times. "Answer," Suzanne ordered, tapping her fingers impatiently on the wall.

But Molly didn't answer. Neither did her machine.

Suzanne slammed the receiver down, then as quickly snapped it up again and dialed the number for Molly's office.

A man answered. "I'm sorry, but Miss Shipwell

has been transferred and is unavailable for calls at the present time.''

''What do you mean, unavailable?'' Suzanne demanded, unnerved. ''And transferred where?''

''I'm sorry, but I am not at liberty to divulge that information.''

Before she could ask any more questions, he hung up.

Her fear turned to panic. Had Molly found out something she wasn't supposed to? Suzanne stared at nothing as her mind spun with unanswered questions and possibilities she didn't want to consider.

She had to talk to Hart. The thought came to her like a lightning bolt cutting through the sky, swift and sure. He'd held her in his arms, kissed her, made love to her. It didn't matter that he'd left without saying anything. He'd probably had duty or a mission or something and just hadn't wanted to wake her.

He'd made love to her—he wasn't the one she had to fear—and if anything had happened to Molly... She couldn't even finish the thought for the anguish it gave her.

''There's not a blemish on the man's record,'' Lewis said, ''unless you call having a wealthy older sister in a Florida retirement home a blemish.''

''A wealthy sister,'' Hart echoed. ''Where'd she get her money?'' He heard the shuffling of paper as Major Lewis flipped through Chief Carger's personnel file.

''I don't know. Maybe it's family money.''

''Then why doesn't the chief have any of it?'' Hart asked.

Lewis sighed. "Captain, have you given any thought to the possibility that maybe you're climbing the wrong tree here?"

Hart's hand tightened involuntarily around the phone receiver. "Maybe, but I don't think so. Carger tried to warn Suzanne Cassidy away from me." He remembered the sensation of a knife piercing his gut when she'd said that, and felt it again now just remembering. He'd always liked the chief. Chalk up another betrayal. "And I don't think it was because he was jealous."

"Maybe his fatherly instincts kicked in," Lewis suggested.

"Yeah, and maybe my halo's on a little crooked," Hart snapped, momentarily losing the grip he had on his temper.

Suzanne's cell phone rang. She tried to dig it out of her purse as she took a corner at thirty-five miles per hour and almost slammed into another car. Shaking, she pulled to the curb and stopped.

"Hello?" she said, flipping open the phone.

"Suz, it's Molly."

"Thank God," Suzanne said, sagging in her seat with relief.

"Listen, I don't have much time," Molly said. "I'm on a pay phone several blocks from my new office. They transferred me."

"I know. I called. But where are you? And why? Was it my fault?"

"It doesn't matter, Suz. Don't worry about it. I'll get my old job back. If I don't, there are probably a few hundred better ones out there. Anyway, listen, what matters right now is that someone knows I was in the corps's classified files and doesn't like it."

Every nerve in Suzanne's body stood on end as apprehension rushed through her.

"I checked those records you wanted me to look at."

"And?" Suzanne said faintly, feeling almost too weak to talk.

"Well, I didn't find anything derogatory on Lane Banner, Zack Morrow or Rand Towler."

Suzanne's nerves frayed further at the names Molly had left out.

"Chief Carger is clean as a whistle—he's never even gotten so much as a parking ticket. Brenner Trent was at Fort Monmouth, like you said, but he didn't pass the Military Intelligence training course. He got booted out."

Trent didn't matter. He was dead.

"And Hart Branson?" Suzanne asked, feeling anticipation and dread squeeze her heart.

"Nothing. Well, no, that's not true. I don't mean 'nothing' like there's nothing there, but 'nothing' like I couldn't pull up anything other than a simple personnel file on him, and that was pretty skimpy. Everything else is classified, like double-0-seven, James Bond kind of classified, as in 'need to know only.'"

Suzanne felt her world tilt further out of her control.

Rick had once told her about a man he'd met who was classified "need to know only." He'd been a government assassin. Her pulses raced.

"I did come across something interesting about

Rick, though,'' Molly went on, jarring Suzanne from her dark thoughts and fearful suspicions.

"About Rick?" she echoed, stupefied.

"Why didn't you mention he'd attended Monmouth, too? I mean, I could have saved myself a lot of time going through records, Suz, if you'd just told me that in the first place.''

"Rick didn't go to Monmouth," Suzanne said.

Molly's laugh was tinged with sarcasm. "Yeah? Well, I beg to differ. Evidently your husband didn't tell you everything, Suz, because his record at State says he definitely did do Military Intelligence training. Uh…''

Suzanne heard the shuffling of paper.

"Here it is," Molly said. "I wrote some of this stuff down. He went to Monmouth three summers ago. Shortly after you two got married.''

Memories swept through Suzanne. They had been married only two weeks when Rick came home one night and said he had to leave the next morning for a six-week training mission. She'd been disappointed and desperately lonely while he'd been gone and had written to him every day, even though he couldn't receive mail.

She'd given him all her letters upon his return, and he'd laughed.

"Not only that," Molly went on, pulling Suzanne from her memories, "but he completed several top-secret assignments before his death, and most of them weren't with the Cobra Corps.''

Could it have been the times he'd said he was taking special-training classes? She tried to think of other times he'd been away from home but not on a mission. Once he'd gone to Washington, but that had been to attend his cousin's wedding. Suzanne hadn't been able to leave work.

Fear rippled through Suzanne like water rippling through rocks strewn across a mountain brook, cold and penetrating. Why had Rick lied to her? How could he have been involved in top-secret assignments without his commanding officers at the corps knowing? Without Hart knowing? Without his own wife knowing?

But maybe Hart had known. Maybe everyone had known but her.

"Molly, I have to go," she said quickly, panic threatening to engulf her. Was Hart MI, too? She remembered the chief telling her that Hart "disappeared" sometimes.

His clearance is Cosmic.

"Thanks for your help, Molly. I'll call you later. At home."

I was the only one who saw Rick die because we'd split into pairs to attack the enemy from different sides, and Rick was my partner.

How much of what Hart had said could she believe?

"No," Molly said hurriedly, "don't call me. I think my phone's bugged. I'll call you."

"Oh, God," Suzanne said, and slapped the cell phone closed.

Run, the voice of fear inside her urged. *Run, now!*

She fought to ignore it. She had to. If she ran from the truth now, she'd never be able to stop. Anyway, there was nowhere to go, nowhere to hide where federal agents intent on getting to her couldn't find her. Hart was her only chance, the only one she could confront with her suspicions and fears, the only one she could demand answers from about her own husband, his past and what Hart knew that he hadn't told her.

If he isn't the guilty one, that same voice of fear whispered tauntingly.

She called the base, but an aide, not Roubechard, refused to tell her where Hart was, stating only that he wasn't in his office. "Would you like to leave a message?" he asked.

She struggled against the panic that tempted her to scream at him. "Tell him to call Suzanne." She gave the aide her cell-phone number and hung up, then dialed the number for Hart's apartment. His answering machine clicked on after the fourth ring.

Her panic heightened, even though she didn't know what she was panicking about.

Her hands trembled.

"Hart, I need to talk to you. I found out—"

The machine cut the connection.

"Blast it all." She redialed the number.

The machine cut the connection again, this time before she could say a word.

Uneasiness niggled at the back of her neck. She put the cell phone down, pulled her car back onto the road and drove directly to his apartment, ignoring the speed limit and thanking the Three Hills police and Arizona state troopers for being busy elsewhere.

She was probably panicking for nothing. He'd most likely just taken the day off. Or maybe he was out on a training exercise. His regular aide hadn't been there. Maybe the one who had been was more of a name-and-serial-number type. Tell no one anything.

What if he'd "disappeared"?

Longing, fear and the prospect of a thousand empty days without him ahead of her sent a chill racing up her spine.

She decided to call the base again. Maybe Roubechard would answer this time.

"Captain Branson's office."

"Private Roubechard?"

"Yes."

Suzanne thanked whatever lucky stars had answered her prayers. "This is Suzanne Cassidy. Is the captain in?"

"Yes, ma'am, just arrived. Can you hold a moment, please?"

Hart answered on the first ring. "Suzanne, what is it?" he demanded. "Is anything wrong?"

"Yes," she said, suddenly wondering again if he was the one behind what was wrong. She tried to push the suspicion from her mind. "We have to talk."

He heard the catch in her voice, the thread of fear and uncertainty. Or was it nervousness? His caution returned. "I was just about to drive over to my place. I left some papers there that I need."

"I'm not far from your apartment," she said. "I'll meet you there."

A few minutes later, Suzanne pulled her car up in front of the sprawling adobe apartment complex. It had been built sometime in the thirties as a residential hotel and playground for Hollywood's rich and famous who'd wanted a little desert sun and a lot of privacy and luxury.

The garage door to Hart's unit was closed, so she couldn't tell if his car was there or not.

She walked past the carefully manicured gardens and heart-shaped swimming pool, the surface of its water glistening brightly beneath the late-morning sun.

She remembered a long ago afternoon. Hart had invited her and Rick, the Trents and several others over. They laughed and talked, swam and barbecued beside the pool. She shrugged away the memory.

His front door was set within a small, Spanish-style, arched portico that afforded it plenty of shade from the sun. Only a few feet from the stoop, she paused, startled to see the door ajar.

A dozen reasons it would be open zipped through her mind, including that he was inside and had left the door open for her. But neither that, nor any of the other reasons she thought of were acceptable. Hart Branson was a man who kept his office locked. He wasn't the type to leave the front door of his home standing open for all the world to enter—for any reason.

She took a cautious step forward. "Hart?" A million dark thoughts rushed through her mind. She lay a hand on the old brass doorknob and leaned past the door, trying to see inside. The blinds were closed and the room was murky with shadows, except for the rectangle of sunlight that streamed onto the beige carpet through the open door. "Hart?" she called again.

Silence was her only answer.

She suddenly noticed a lamp lying on the floor, its shade half-crushed. Nearby several books had been swept from a bookcase to the floor. Fear seized her in its claws, sending a shower of goose bumps over her flesh and leaving her trembling with visions of possibilities she didn't want to imagine, but did.

He could be hurt. Maybe he'd fallen and hit his head. Maybe someone... The thought propelled her into the apartment. She peered into the kitchen, then hurried toward the bedroom. "Hart?"

She sensed movement behind her and started to turn.

Something hard slammed against the side of her head. Stars and brightness instantly filled her mind, and weakness seized her legs. Then darkness swept over her, and she fell to the floor.

The five-car pileup on the highway leading out of town, and to Hart's apartment, had delayed him by almost an hour.

He looked for her car in the visitors' area when he pulled in, but didn't see it.

Most likely she'd gotten tired of waiting for him and thought he'd stood her up. Maybe she'd driven out to the base. He walked to his apartment and as he approached noticed that the blinds on his front window were closed. He always left them partially open.

Most likely he'd forgotten. He slipped his key into the doorknob and found it wasn't locked. That was something he hadn't forgotten. He instantly tensed and wished the small gun lying in the drawer of his nightstand was in his hand, instead. Hart pushed the door open with his foot, but remained on the stoop, listening.

Nothing.

The apartment was filled with shadows. He reached around the doorjamb and flipped the light switch. Several old wall sconces illuminated the room. Shock and disbelief held him momentarily on the spot. Either a raging tornado had hit the inside of his apartment, or someone had done one hell of a thorough job of searching it.

Half the cushions in the living room had been slashed open. Tables were lying on their sides, chairs upturned. Every drawer in the kitchen was open, contents scattered, and the bedroom was even worse.

It looked like a war zone.

"Son of a..." Shock gave way to fury. The last time it had been by professionals who had taken care to leave things as near to the way they'd found them as possible. This time whoever had searched his place hadn't cared that he'd know. He'd blamed the feds before, and this could be their work, too. Maybe they were looking for whatever copies of the stolen plans hadn't been sold yet and, if so, didn't care what they had to do or destroy to get to them.

But as quickly as the thought came to him, he dismissed it. Instinct and experience told him this hadn't been done by professionals. This had been done by someone who hated him.

He remembered the man in the restaurant who'd played a coin through his fingers and watched Suzanne. He remembered Salvatore DeBraggo—the bereaved widower who was really a fed; Chief Carger, who had warned Suzanne that Hart would only end up hurting her; and Rick, who was supposed to be dead, but who the feds believed wasn't.

The phone rang, but it took a minute for Hart to find it beneath the mound of bed covers and clothes that had been tossed to the floor on top of it.

"Branson," he said automatically.

"Sir, it's Roubechard."

"What the hell is it, Roubechard?"

"Well, sir, I, um, don't know if it means anything, but I just discovered that a week before the Jaguar Loop mission Lieutenant Brenner Trent's wife filed for a divorce."

Worlds collided as memories washed over Hart.

It's over, Hart. For good. Suzanne and I are getting a divorce.

Almost the last words Rick had said to him echoed through Hart's mind.

Suzanne had asked for a divorce, and Rick was dead. Kristen Trent had filed for a divorce, and Brenner Trent was dead.

Could that be a coincidence? Cold skepticism drew at his thoughts. He didn't believe in coincidence. Things happened in life, good or bad, for a reason, usually in reaction to someone else's action. Sometimes the connections weren't readily identifiable, but they were always there.

All of Hart's suspicions assaulted him anew, stronger and deeper, refusing to be vanquished no matter how much his heart tried to deny them.

But he would have known—while making love to her—if her tears were a lie. Wouldn't he?

Anger, frustration and resentment filled him. He had to find the truth. If she was guilty, he'd spend the rest of his life missing her—and damning her.

If she was innocent, he had to save her.

Either way, he had to know.

"Roubechard," he said, his tone hard and determined, "did you get Rick Cassidy's autopsy report?"

"No, sir. I've sent three requests, sir, but they keep being denied."

"Call Major Lewis. I asked him to try, too. See if he got anywhere on it. And pull together anything else you can get your hands on involving Lieutenant Cassidy. And I want the same on Brenner Trent— he was killed last year. Find out what you can about his wife, too. Hell, check their whole families while you're at it."

"Yes, sir."

"And I want that information on my desk when I get there," Hart said. "Which will be shortly."

"Yes, sir."

He slammed the phone down and looked around the bedroom again, his anger edging toward rage. There was no more time to waste. He needed to talk to the fed who was supposedly watching him and Suzanne. DeBraggo. Maybe he'd seen who had done this. Or maybe *he'd* done it. But first Hart had to know how to contact the man.

He grabbed the phone and started to punch out the number for the senator's aide...then noticed the dark-crimson stain on the carpet. He put down the phone and dropped to his knees, then touched a finger to the stain. Blood. He looked around, his heart racing, his mind refusing to consider even for a second that it could be Suzanne's blood on the carpet.

She should have been here before him. What if she'd walked in on someone?

The phone rang again.

"Brigade Commander Dellos just called, sir," Roubechard said without preamble.

Dellos. Not someone Hart wanted to hear from.

He was pretty certain he knew what Roubechard's next words would be.

"You're to report to the Pentagon in twenty-four hours, sir."

Dammit. He'd been right. It could be a summons to receive special instructions for a meeting or a highly classified mission, but something told Hart it was more likely to do with the feds, Suzanne and the stolen plans. Which meant he'd just about run out of time as far as proving Suzanne and himself innocent.

"Roubechard," he said, "find Brenner Trent's widow, then send a couple of MPs to pick her up and bring her to my office for questioning. And tell them not to take no for an answer." He glanced down at the bloodstain again and felt a chill of alarm. "Get the police to my apartment. Tell them it was broken into and there's blood on the floor." His heart raced. "And send someone to get Suzanne Cassidy. Now!"

"Yes, sir."

"I'll be there in thirty."

He hung up, then immediately picked up the phone again and punched out Suzanne's number. Her answering machine came on.

"Suzanne," he said, after the beep, "are you there? Pick up, it's Hart. Suzanne?" He waited, drumming his fingers on the nightstand, staring down at the stain on the carpet, feeling his nerves fray further with the passing of each silent second. "Suzanne!"

He slammed the phone down again, then fought to get control of his emotions. She'd probably just gotten angry when he didn't show up and had gone off to do something else, he told himself. Or maybe she was on her way to the base or back to the bungalow.

Hart glanced at the spot of blood again. Maybe whoever ransacked the place had cut himself on something.

It was a nice theory, but it didn't convince him. Tension pulled at his bones, strained his muscles and filled him with alarm. And fear.

Then he remembered the senator saying that both he and Suzanne were being watched by the feds. A sense of relief eased some of his tension. Nothing could happen to her if the feds were watching. She wasn't really alone.

The memory of Suzanne in his arms, her naked body pressed to his, reacting to his every touch, his every caress, tore at him. For the past several years every dream he'd ever had, every fantasy, had centered around Suzanne. Whether he'd liked it or not or even wanted to acknowledge it, she was a part of his life forever.

Chapter 13

Hart changed into a fresh uniform and made it to the base in twenty minutes, walking into the office only a moment before the MP sent to pick up Suzanne returned.

"She wasn't home, sir," the MP said. "None of the neighbors had seen her."

Hart had expected that, since she hadn't answered the phone. "I was going to check the other places your aide mentioned, but I found this note tacked to her front door, sir, and figured I'd better get it to you." He handed Hart a folded piece of paper.

Hart glanced at the heavily scrawled message.

Come to the Old Tucson Studios tonight at midnight—alone, or you will never see Suzanne Cassidy alive again.

A chill of fear and guilt crept up his spine.

He read the note again.

It could be a trap meant to lure him somewhere alone—so that they could kill him and set him up to take the fall for the feds—and Suzanne could be the willing bait.

Or this threat could be on the level, and they would kill her if he didn't do as ordered.

Hart swore.

The other men feigned deafness.

He could have prevented this if he'd placed a guard on her earlier. Whether he'd believed her or not, he should have taken precautions.

And where the hell had her guardian fed been?

He crumpled the note in his fist and stared at nothing, his thoughts churning. Suddenly, unable to explain it even to himself, he knew, in his heart, that she was innocent.

Whatever wrongs had been done, she hadn't done them.

With that conviction, the icy calm of battle and determination invaded his veins. He'd participated in too many dangerous missions to be foolish enough to believe that if he followed her abductors' instructions and went after Suzanne alone, either one of them would survive. Most likely they'd both be killed and evidence left on them to convince the feds they were the traitors.

If Suzanne wasn't dead already.

The phone rang. Roubechard ran into his office. "It's Ms. Cassidy." It was his private line. Hart grabbed for the phone on his desk.

"Hart?"

"Suzanne, where are you? Are you all right?"

"Yes, I don't know, I think so." The gash on her

head from where she'd been hit was still throbbing, but at least it had stopped bleeding. She tried not to look at the man standing before her. How could she have been so utterly stupid?

She reached up, touched the lump on her head and winced. "Hart, I was at your place... The door was open and I knew that wasn't like you. I was afraid something had happened to you, so I went in and..." She paused, trying to think of some way to tell him who'd attacked her.

The man standing before her nudged her shoulder roughly, his way of encouraging her to keep talking.

Suzanne felt a flash of pain in her head. "Oh, damn," she wailed, and closed her eyes against the lightning bolts that shot from the bump on her head straight through her brain and down to her toes.

"Suzanne?" Fear gripped Hart.

"Sorry," she said weakly. "They hit me over the head at your place and..."

Hart remembered the blood on his carpet.

"Suzanne, do you know where you are?"

"No. They let me call you, but— Ow," she screamed as the phone was suddenly wrenched from her hand.

"But you won't see her alive again if you don't follow our instructions," a deep voice said into Hart's ear. "Midnight. The Old Tucson Studios. Alone."

"Listen, you bas—"

An ugly laugh cut off Hart's words, then the line went dead.

"Dammit!" he roared, and hung up the phone. He paced the length of the room. The thought that she could already be dead had been enough to threaten the beat of his heart, take the breath from his lungs and the strength from his limbs, which meant he had tried not to let himself even consider the possibility.

Now…they'd let her talk to him so that he'd know there was still hope, so that he'd follow their instructions.

But now that they knew he would come, they could kill her. Icy hands of fear wrapped around his heart and threatened to never let go. But along with fear came rage, firing the adrenaline of battle within him.

"Roubechard, find Lieutenants Morrow and Towler and get them here on the double."

Rick's death had reminded Hart why he'd never wanted friends, and when Suzanne walked out of his life, the pain of loss had deepened. He'd tried to close himself off again, but Zack and Rand had refused to let him withdraw completely. Now they remained the only two people he even came close to trusting, the only two people who dared to be his friends.

His thoughts spun. What if the feds had been right all along and Suzanne was guilty, the phone call merely another ploy? What if this was a trap?

Everything in him resisted the idea.

For the first time Hart began to question himself. Was it possible he was wrong, that in spite of what he'd seen, Rick hadn't died in that crash? It would explain the feds' suspicions of Suzanne.

But there was another possibility. Rumors had once flown that Rick and Kristen Trent had had an affair. What if the rumors had been true and now—

Roubechard returned. "They're on their way, sir.

And a clerk just delivered this.'' He handed Hart a large envelope.

He glanced at it, ready to dismiss it as something that could wait, maybe forever if tonight went all wrong. Then the stamp of the coroner's office in one corner of the envelope caught his attention.

The autopsy report on Rick.

Hart tore open the envelope and his blood turned cold as he quickly scanned the autopsy report on Rick Cassidy. Positive identification had been inconclusive.

A knock on the door interrupted his shock.

An MP entered and saluted. ''Captain Branson, we weren't able to locate Mrs. Trent, sir.''

Hart glared at the man, angry with everyone now. Was Trent's widow just out somewhere, innocently going about her business, or was she in on this thing?

Zack and Rand walked into his office and saluted.

''At ease,'' Hart said.

They approached his desk. ''What's up?'' Zack asked. ''Roub said it was urgent.''

''It is. I need your help.''

''Then you need mine, too,'' Salvatore DeBraggo said, walking into Hart's office and flashing his badge.

''Sorry, sir,'' Roubechard said hurriedly, following the man. ''I tried to tell him you were in a meeting and he'd have to wait or come back at another time, but he just walked past me and—''

Hart bolted to his feet, fury washing over him. ''Help? You were supposed to be watching her,'' Hart growled. He glared at DeBraggo as an urge to

rip the man's throat out threatened to consume him.
"Instead, you let them take her."

"I didn't let them *do* anything," DeBraggo
snarled back, dark eyes flashing. "She went into
your place, and I followed her. For my trouble
someone damned near split my skull in two."

Hart noticed for the first time that the back of the
man's head was covered by a large white bandage,
but it didn't make him feel any better, didn't soothe
his anger.

"Did you see them?" he demanded.

"Yes, one of them, though it was the one we'd
already figured was in on this thing."

"Who?" Hart snapped.

"Carger."

"The chief?" Zack said, looking from Hart to
DeBraggo.

"What's going on, Captain?" Rand asked calmly.

Hart stared at DeBraggo. "You're sure it was
Carger?"

"Do I look Spanish?" DeBraggo sneered sarcastically. He reached beneath his jacket.

Rand, Zack and the MP all lunged forward and
grabbed him.

"I'm FBI," DeBraggo said angrily, flashing his
badge again.

The three men stepped back, and DeBraggo
poured a couple of aspirin into his hand from the
bottle he'd pulled from his pocket. He downed them
without water.

"Look," he said, "the bureau suspected Suzanne
Cassidy of treason and figured you might be in on
it, but had no proof. Still doesn't."

"And what do you and your buddies at the bureau

suspect now?'' Hart challenged. ''That I kidnapped Suzanne and this is some kind of strategic move on our parts?''

Sal DeBraggo smiled coldly. ''What my cohorts at the bureau suspect now, Captain, is that your girlfriend is either in one hell of a lot of trouble, or the two of you are the most cunning pair of thieves and murderers we've ever run up against.''

''Murderers?'' Zack echoed, his eyes widening. ''Would somebody explain, please?''

Rand nudged him. ''Shut up.''

DeBraggo shrugged. ''Someone went down in Cassidy's chopper, Captain. And we know it was sabotaged. We've known that ever since the retrieval team found the wreckage. But IDing the body was impossible. So, we figured either it was Cassidy in that bird and he was murdered, or he's alive and some other poor sap was snuffed in order to take his place. Either way, murder.''

''Why are you telling me all this,'' Hart asked, no more willing to trust DeBraggo than he would a rat, ''if you still suspect me?''

''Because,'' DeBraggo replied, ''that's not my favorite scenario. Lieutenant Cassidy reported the theft of plans before he took off. Why do that if he was going to steal them?''

''To divert suspicion,'' Hart said.

DeBraggo shrugged. ''Maybe. But it also focused attention on him. No, I believe that it was Lieutenant Cassidy who was killed, his wife knows absolutely nothing and you told the truth when you said you saw his chopper hit and explode and he was killed. You've got a clean and pretty damned good record and don't seem the type to commit espionage and murder. Especially since the guy murdered was your best, and seemingly only, friend.''

"Thanks," Hart muttered.

"The problem is, the bureau doesn't have any other good suspects. That's where I came in. My plan was devised to rout out some other suspects, if there were any."

"What plan?"

"We figured Ms. Cassidy would run to you for help if she thought she was really in trouble and it had to do with her late husband, you and the army. Especially since the only other person she could have gone to was her cousin at the State Department, and we made sure her cousin wasn't reachable."

"Thought of everything, didn't you?" Hart said, derision coloring his tone.

"No," DeBraggo said, suddenly sounding half-beaten, "we didn't think they'd nab her."

For the next two hours they filled Zack and Rand in and planned Suzanne's rescue—or, if they were all wrong and she didn't need one, Hart's rescue.

Hart glanced at his watch. Everyone was in place and ready. It was almost midnight. He moved away from the Old Tucson Studios entry gate and climbed over the adjacent fence. Dropping to the ground, he hunkered down low, the night-vision goggles he wore allowing him to see as if it were daylight. He scanned the area, seeing no one, then moved down the dark street, staying close to the old adobe-and-wood buildings, thankful there was only a sliver of moon in the sky.

John Wayne, Gary Cooper, Henry Fonda—they'd all walked this same street at one time or another, a six-gun strapped to their hips, danger lurking around every corner. But that had been for the cameras.

This was real.

An old steam locomotive, its armor glistening beneath the pale moonlight, sat beside the dark railroad depot. Nearby a stagecoach stood empty next to a corral.

Hart had no idea which building Suzanne and her abductors were in, which gave them the advantage.

Hart turned a corner and stopped as he saw light shining from the windows of the old ranch house that had been used in the television series *The High Chaparral.* He'd seen it several times on late-night television. It was one of Zack's favorites.

The house sat on a slight rise.

Suzanne's abductors had obviously felt no need to hide their presence.

There was little around the house in the way of cover for Hart to use while approaching. He pulled a two-way radio from a pocket of his combat vest and called in. ''Ice to Cowboy.''

''Cowboy, here,'' Zack said.

''They're in the High Chaparral house.''

''Perfect place for a showdown,'' Cowboy said. ''Be there in five. Over.''

Hart removed his goggles. Crouching as close to the ground as he could, he made his way toward the house, praying no one would see him. He stopped behind a large crate that stood just a few feet from the front porch and peered around it into one of the windows.

The man who'd been watching Suzanne in the restaurant and playing the coin through his fingers walked past, then walked back and looked out.

Something had bothered Hart about Rick's autopsy report, but he hadn't been able to determine what. Now, suddenly, he knew. He stared at the man from the restaurant, trying to see beyond the plastic surgery he suspected had been performed over the last year. But it was too good. There was not even a trace of the face of the man he'd once known.

Tearing his gaze away, he looked beyond the man into the room. He saw the chief seated on a bench and leaning back against the wall, feet up on a table. He looked as if he didn't have a care in the world. Fury pulled at Hart's fists, drew at his jaw, rolled through his blood. Carger would have all too many cares when this was over.

Trent's widow and Suzanne were sitting nearby. The widow appeared to be asleep, and Suzanne was staring at the chief.

Prisoner? Or accomplice? The thought jumped into Hart's mind, but it was one he didn't welcome.

Suzanne turned then and said something to the chief.

Carger didn't respond, but the man at the window turned and stalked across the room, stopping in front of her, his stance emanating rage.

Hart tensed.

Suzanne spoke again, then thrust out her chin defiantly, as if daring him to respond.

The man slapped her across the face.

She flew back in her chair, hit the wall and nearly fell from her seat.

Hart jumped up, fury boiling his blood, then caught himself and moved back into the shadows behind the crate. He'd kill the creep, but not yet. To move in now would only result in them both getting killed. He glanced at his watch.

One minute.

Time to move closer.

He ran stealthily to the veranda, straightening upon arrival and flattening himself against the rough adobe wall beside one of the windows.

He could hear them talking now, arguing about whether or not he was coming and what to do if he didn't.

Wop-wop-wop.

Hart glanced toward the sky as the soft but still-distant sound of rotor blades cut through the night's silence, announcing the approach of two Cobras and several Blackhawks.

He moved around a corner of the house and positioned himself nearer one of the side windows.

Wop-wop-wop.

The sound grew louder, deafening. The Cobras flew into sight.

The two men inside ran to the door, threw it open and stepped onto the veranda to look up past the overhanging roof.

"Damned double-crossing SOB," Carger cursed, flicking his cigarette into the darkness.

Eight ropes hit the ground—four in front of the house, four to the rear. Almost instantly eight paratroopers descended from the Blackhawks. The two Cobras hovered overhead, standing guard, while a gunner in each Blackhawk trained his sights on the house.

Hart took a running leap and threw himself through a side window, rolled on the floor, then jumped to his feet, his gun gripped and ready in his hand.

Carger and the other man whirled and ran back inside. Carger headed for the back door, the other man grabbed for Suzanne. But she evaded his grasp and dashed toward Hart.

"Get down," he yelled, and shoved her behind him, turning back to face his adversary at the same time.

"Say goodbye to the world, Captain," the man said. His gun was pointed directly at Hart.

Suzanne saw the hate in his eyes and knew he was going to kill Hart. She threw herself at him to ward off the bullet.

Glass splintered.

Men yelled.

Gunfire exploded in the room.

And Suzanne screamed.

Her assailant suddenly jerked awkwardly and dropped his gun. Blood spurted from his shoulder as he fell to his knees.

Near one of the other windows Zack stood, brushing glass from his flight suit, while Rand ushered Chief Carger and the widow Trent back into the room.

"Everything okay, Captain?" Zack asked, grinning as he glanced down at the wounded man.

Hart waved at Zack and pulled Suzanne into his arms, knowing he needed to hold her, to feel her against him in order to believe that she was really all right. He had never been so afraid or so angry. She could have been killed.

Relief swept through Suzanne as she sank into Hart's embrace. He'd come for her—and he was safe. Whatever else happened, that was all that mattered now. She held him to her, the warmth of his body banishing the icy chill of fear that had kept her mercilessly in its grip for the past several hours. They were alive. The world was still spinning. This horrible ordeal was finally over. Everything was going to be—

"Hart," she screamed, tearing herself from his arms and staring past him.

He spun.

The wounded man struggled to his feet, holding a hand to his bloody shoulder. "I knew I should have killed you during Jaguar Loop, too," he growled. Hate shone from his eyes.

Rage sped through Hart like fire sweeping over a field of dry grass. Stalking across the room, he grabbed the front of the man's shirt and jerked him toward him. "Your face is that of a stranger," he said softly, "but we both know who you are, don't we?"

In spite of his words, there was one thing he had to do to be certain he was right. Stepping back, Hart ripped the front of the man's shirt away.

Suzanne stared, not understanding.

Hart's gaze turned murderous.

The night before the Jaguar Loop mission, the pilots had been playing volleyball in an effort to relieve the tension. Brenner Trent had been taking bets on which side would win.

Just before the end of the game Rick ran to make a hit and tripped. The dead tree limb he fell on had ripped a nasty gash halfway across his chest, but he had adamantly refused to see the medic for fear he'd be pulled from the mission. Rick could have had plastic surgery to fix his face, but why would he bother with a scar on his chest no one would see?

Hart glanced at the man's chest, at where there should be a scar if this was Rick Cassidy. There wasn't. His gaze shot up to meet the cold blue eyes staring defiantly back at him.

"You lousy son of a bitch," he said softly, then turned away from Brenner Trent and walked back to Suzanne.

"I told you this wouldn't work, Brenner," Kristen yelled as Sal DeBraggo secured a pair of handcuffs around her wrists. "I told you. But you just wouldn't listen, would you?"

Suzanne glanced at DeBraggo, then looked at the man Kristen Trent had called Brenner. Understanding flashed through her instantly. He looked nothing like the boyish soldier she remembered. Instead, his features were sharply chiseled, every line hard and unyielding.

Suzanne shivered, knowing how close death had come and how thankful she was that it hadn't.

DeBraggo looked over Kristen's shoulder at Hart. "From now on, Captain, I'll do my rescuing from ground level."

Zack laughed. "He didn't take much to my flying, I guess."

Kristen and the two men were ushered outside and toward the Blackhawks waiting in the parking lot.

Hart turned back to Suzanne. "Are you all right?" he asked, drawing her back into his arms. He'd been a fool for not believing her, for letting her walk away from him a year ago, and he hadn't realized it until it was almost too late.

She nodded, her head against his chest. "I was so scared they were going to kill you."

Emotion overwhelmed him, but rather than push it away, as he'd always done in the past, he welcomed it. "And I was terrified they'd already killed you."

"But—" she shook her head "—I don't understand. Why is Mr. DeBraggo here?"

"He's a fed," Hart said. "I found out a couple of days ago. He's been watching you, and me, ever since you arrived here. The bit about his wife and the jewelry was a cover. He borrowed it from the New York Met. His job was to watch you and protect you if necessary."

"Protect me? I thought they wanted to put me in jail."

"He used us to ferret out the real murderers and thieves."

"Then Rick really is…"

"Dead. Carger stole the plans from his attaché, and Brenner sabotaged Rick's Cobra so everyone would think the plans were destroyed in the wreckage. What they didn't know was that Rick had already discovered the theft and reported it. Which is the reason DeBraggo never went along with the idea of Rick being alive."

"So they didn't have to kill him."

"No, they didn't."

His arms felt so good around her. She breathed in the smell of him, snuggled into his warmth, drew on his strength.

"But how did you know that was Brenner Trent? I mean, his face…it was so changed. He didn't look at all like himself."

Hart felt a sudden weight settle on him. Her question was the one he'd hoped she wouldn't ask and the one he'd known he would have to answer, anyway. "I saw him in the restaurant watching you the day you went to meet Kristen Trent."

"What?" She pulled back slightly and looked up at him. "You were there?"

"Yes. I didn't know it was Brenner then," Hart said. "But I knew, somehow, that he was someone I knew and involved in this whole mess."

She pushed out of his embrace, as he'd feared she would. "You followed me. You saw him watching me." She shook her head. "Why didn't you tell me? Why didn't you warn me?"

Hart inhaled deeply and sighed. She'd hate him now, also as he'd feared. "I didn't know if I could trust you. I didn't know if he was watching you or your back, whether he was a federal agent, an enemy or an accomplice."

"*My* accomplice," she said, nodding in understanding.

"Yes." He felt as if he was digging his own grave. "I hated suspecting you, Suzanne, but I had to. And I only figured out this whole mess a few hours ago with DeBraggo's help. But by then it was too late. Brenner and Carger already had you."

Suddenly the joy of being in his arms, of feeling the warmth and strength of his embrace and knowing she was safe was gone. Instead, Suzanne felt cold and empty and very much alone.

Tears filled her eyes, and anguish her heart. "I was terrified," she said, her voice breaking over the words. "I was terrified for you, Hart, at the thought of you coming after me and being killed."

"But I did come," he said softly, trying to reason with her, "and I didn't get killed."

Fury swept through her, engulfed her, unreasonably, inexplicably and uncontrollably. "Yes, you came, but you thought I'd lied to you. You suspected me of treason and murder. And you probably still weren't sure if I was innocent or luring you into a trap until you got here, were you?"

He didn't answer, but his silence was answer enough.

"You didn't tell me about him." She pointed in the direction Brenner had been taken. "You didn't tell me and I was nearly killed."

"I couldn't trust you."

For several seconds that seemed longer than an eternity, yet shorter than the blink of an eye, she stared at him, looking for the man she'd thought she had known, thought she had fallen in love with. But he wasn't there. Maybe he had never been there, except in her desperate, lonely, yearning imagination.

"How could you do that?" Her eyes glistened now with tears, but without waiting for an answer she turned and stormed from the house.

Hart walked to the door and watched her stride down the narrow, dirt-covered street toward the police cars that had joined the Blackhawks and Cobras sitting quiet and still in the parking lot.

Ever since the day she'd left Three Hills, he had felt an emptiness inside he couldn't banish, no matter what he did. He'd tried immersing himself in work, dating a different woman every week, and a few times he'd even tried to drown himself in booze. Nothing had worked. But he'd denied that the way he'd felt was because of anything other than the knowledge that the only friend he'd ever allowed himself to have was dead.

Now he knew it had been more than that. It had been because Suzanne had left, because she hadn't been in his life anymore.

He watched her pass through the studio's entry gate and out of his sight, and the old, familiar feeling of chilling emptiness that had started to steal over him again intensified.

Hart sighed deeply and walked into the yard. He looked up at the sky. It was better this way. Clenching his hands into fists, he repeated the conviction, over and over. It was better this way. Love was merely a fantasy, and it always died or betrayed you somehow. The attraction that had burned between them had only been physical, anyway. They'd have soon tired of each other. Maybe even ended up hating each other. Wasn't that what happened to most people?

He walked toward one of the waiting Blackhawks.

Zack approached him as he was about to climb in. "The C.O. just called," he said. "He wants you to report to the base and assist with an immediate interrogation of the prisoners."

Hart nodded. Why not? He didn't have anything else to do.

Chapter 14

Suzanne grabbed another handful of lingerie from the dresser drawer and threw it into her suitcase. "Damn him." She stalked to the closet, ripped another dress from its hanger, threw it into the suitcase, slammed the thing shut and swore again.

"Fry in hell, Captain Branson," she said, damning the tears that had begun to course down her cheeks as she'd walked away from him and still wouldn't stop.

She grabbed another suitcase, then paused upon catching a glimpse of herself in the dresser mirror. "Oh, God," she moaned. Who was she trying to fool? In Hart Branson's embrace she'd found what she'd been seeking all her life, what she'd always dreamed and fantasized about, what she'd wanted so desperately to feel. She'd found a love so all-consuming she didn't know if she could live without it.

But he hadn't trusted her. He'd almost gotten her killed.

Walking into the living room, she flopped down on the overstuffed sofa and stared past the glass patio doors at the distant horizon, trying to deny to herself that she'd been waiting for him to call.

The mountains in the far-off distance were ragged silhouettes against the dark sky, the stars above them like tiny diamonds.

She glanced at the old pioneer clock that sat on the mantel. It was four in the morning, three hours since she'd left him at the studio lot. Plenty of time for him to have called. She drew up her legs and wrapped her arms around them.

How could she have been so stupid as to fall in love with Hart? He was the exact type of man she'd sworn never to even throw a second glance at again. His life was devoted to the military, and danger. Two things she could definitely do without forever.

Her father had been career army. Her husband had been career army. They'd loved the danger, the constant moving, the new assignments, never knowing what tomorrow would bring.

If her father hadn't been so devoted to the army— had loved his wife and daughter more—maybe they would have remained a family. Maybe her mother wouldn't have changed husbands as often as the wind changed direction.

And maybe if she hadn't married a man so much like her father, the marriage would have worked. Maybe if she could have gotten Rick to leave the army—have a normal job—a normal life—he wouldn't have cheated on her. Maybe—

You didn't lose them because they were army, a little voice in the back of her mind said.

She refused to listen and shoved off the sofa to pace the room. Why did the men in her life always betray her?

Hart had believed her capable of treason. And murder. It was incredible. Preposterous. Yet he had. He had talked to her, laughed with her, kissed her and made love to her, and all the while he'd believed her a murderer.

She suddenly stopped pacing. He had believed it of her—and at the same time, she had believed it of him. The shock of that realization stunned her.

She was guilty of the same thing she was damning him for.

But if he loved her, why had he let her walk away? Why hadn't he called?

Hart walked out of the room they'd been using to interrogate Brenner and his accomplice. Exhaustion pulled at every muscle and bone in his body. He pushed open the exit door and walked outside. Stretching his arms wide, he breathed deeply of the fresh night air and drank in the sweet smell of the desert.

But it didn't take away the feeling of emptiness that had been gnawing at him for hours, and going back to his apartment was far from appealing. The place was still trashed, and Military Intelligence agents were probably still there, looking for anything Brenner or Carger might have tried to plant to incriminate him.

The personnel-file notation that Brenner Trent had failed intelligence training had been a cover. He'd been planted in the Cobra Corps by Military Intelligence as a security watchdog when plans were first developed to use the experimental weapons-detection system in one of the corps's missions. They were afraid of a leak, and it had been Brenner's job to make certain that if there was one, it was silenced immediately.

Just before Jaguar Loop, however, Trent's wife had threatened to divorce him.

Brenner knew his wife was tired of just getting by on his military pay, of never having any of life's luxuries, and he'd suspected Kristen was having an affair with Rick. But he hadn't confronted her for fear of losing her. He'd panicked when she'd asked for the divorce, then decided she was leaving him for Rick, because even though most people didn't know it, Rick's family had money, which meant Rick had money. Brenner thought if he could find a way to give Kristen the kind of life she wanted, if he could buy her the expensive things she craved, she'd stay with him.

And it had almost worked.

He'd drafted Chief Carger into his plans—a man on the verge of retirement. The only thing Carger had in life was his meager military retirement and an older sister living in a retirement home, her mind gone to Alzheimer's disease. She had inherited a lot of money from her husband, but was nowhere near death's door.

After Rick's chopper crashed, the brass had decided he was their most likely suspect, especially when his body and what was left of the chopper couldn't be retrieved until months after the mission was over.

And that had fit perfectly into Brenner's plan.

The government's suspicions had seemed confirmed when positive identification of Rick's body had been inconclusive.

When there was no public mention of the stolen secrets, Trent thought he'd gotten away with his scheme. But he'd known it would be too risky to sell the plans right away, so he'd waited, then executed his own death, had plastic surgery and, finally, found a buyer.

But panic seized him when an FBI agent visited his "widow," who'd planned to join him in Europe once they'd disposed of the last of the plans. Brenner feared the feds had finally turned their suspicions on him. But it was Chief Carger who'd gotten the brilliant idea to resurrect a dead man to take the blame, along with his very much alive wife.

Brenner's widow had impersonated Suzanne and opened the bank account. The European spy had merely been a stroke of luck for them, and a real customer for Suzanne, recommended by, as it turned out, Robert Marsei.

And she'd had no idea who Robert Marsei really was.

Brenner Trent had thought of everything. Except that Suzanne would run to Hart for help.

Hart was halfway back to his office when he detoured toward the airstrip. Silence hung over everything, and he welcomed it.

Climbing into his Cobra, he felt the tension drain from his body for the first time in hours. He laid his head back on the seat and watched as the first rays of the morning sun began to peek over the horizon.

He wanted Suzanne more than he ever thought it possible to want a woman.

A long sigh, almost like a surrender, shuddered from deep inside him.

He'd never believed in love, had damned it and tried to deny it, but he could no longer deny that for whatever little it was worth, Suzanne Cassidy had stolen his heart and he'd unconsciously given her his trust when he'd charged into that room to save her.

He almost laughed aloud in derision of his thoughts.

His heart and his trust.

Those were the two things he'd always vowed never to give wholly to anyone, because they were the two things he knew he couldn't get back, no matter how desperately he wanted to or how hard he tried.

And he had unwittingly given them to her.

He thought about all the reasons he'd tried to deny his feelings for her, all the reasons he'd told himself he would never love anyone, and suddenly those reasons seemed frail and hollow.

He'd been afraid to love her because he'd been afraid she would betray him. Instead, she came to him for help, trusted him to save her and had almost gotten herself killed trying to save him.

She had never betrayed him, and unless he was the world's biggest fool, he knew now she never would.

Sliding back the Cobra's canopy, Hart climbed out.

It was time to stop being afraid.

* * *

Suzanne had known she'd find him at the airfield once she realized he wasn't at his office or apartment. But it had taken all her courage to come.

He had never said he loved her, never made any promises of a future for them together, but she'd finally admitted to herself it was what she wanted.

If he didn't want the same thing, she needed to see that in his eyes, needed to hear him say it to her. Then she would go back to Los Angeles and never contact him again.

She paused as she saw him climb from the Cobra, then turn toward her. Nervousness and fear seized her. Was she merely being a fool again? What if he had never said he loved her because he didn't love her? Did she really want to hear that? Could she stand to hear that?

No, a little voice inside of her wailed. But her feet kept moving forward, taking her to him.

Hart turned and saw Suzanne walking across the tarmac toward him, and for a brief second he thought he was imagining her there because he so desperately wanted her to be there. He stood still, afraid to move for fear she would disappear, and watched her close the distance between them.

Myriad emotions assaulted him anew, but the one he felt the deepest, the one only a short time ago he swore he would never feel for another human being but now felt for her, was love. Deep, stirring, desperate, and all-consuming.

Suddenly fear swept through him. She had come to say goodbye. The conviction sent a chill racing through him like nothing he'd ever felt before.

He turned away. If he didn't look, she wouldn't

be there. If she wasn't there, she couldn't say good-bye again. He'd lost her once, and now he knew he couldn't stand to lose her again.

Suzanne saw him look away and uncertainty seized her. He was in silhouette to her now, the rising sun at his back like a brilliant golden halo, surrounding him, obscuring his face, his eyes and leaving her unable to determine whether he was glad to see her or wished she hadn't come.

How would she ever endure all the long hours of the future without him if he didn't want her?

She should leave. Now, before it was too late and she made a fool of herself.

Her steps faltered and she paused.

Hart saw her pause, saw her start to turn away, and anxiety overwhelmed him.

Now or never, a voice in the back of his mind said.

Impulse melded with his desire, want overrode caution, need swept away fear. Before he could reconsider his action, he closed the distance between them and swept her into his arms.

"I've been a fool," he said gruffly, holding her to him, crushing her against his body, needing to feel her flesh against his.

She shook her head. "Hart…"

She had come to say goodbye. His fear deepened and pushed him on. "I always believed love was nothing more than an illusion, Suzanne, a fantasy that would never last, an emotion that could only lead to certain betrayal and pain."

"Hart," Suzanne said, touched by his words, by his arms around her, the look of need and longing she saw shining in his eyes. "I—"

"And trust was something I didn't dare give anyone," he went on, the words spilling from his lips in a rush. "But I was wrong," he said quickly, cutting her off when she tried to respond, afraid of what she had been about to say. "I know I was wrong. I know because I know now that I love you. It's not an illusion, not a fantasy. I love you more than life, Suzanne, more than anything in the world…"

She couldn't say goodbye. He wouldn't let her.

"…and if the hardened military side of me hadn't known you were innocent all along, dammit—" tears filled his eyes as anguish cut at his voice and turned it to a ragged whisper "—my heart did. I swear, Suzanne, my heart always believed in you."

"Hart," she whispered again, tears shimmering in her eyes now.

Fear held his heart in its grip. She was going to say goodbye. She was crying because she couldn't love him, and he didn't want to hear that. "I need you in my life, Suzanne." He had never pleaded with anyone for anything, but now he was pleading for his life. "I love you, Suzanne, and I want you in my life. Forever."

"And I want to be there," she said, touching his cheek ever so lightly with her fingertips. "I want to be there. Forever."

He couldn't believe what he'd heard. "I'll love you forever," he said, "prove to you every day that you are the most important thing in my life."

She remembered all the doubts and suspicions she'd had about him and smiled. "I love you, Captain Branson," she said simply, then drew his head down and captured his lips with hers.

Feelings surged within Hart that for the first time in his life he had no desire to deny, no urge to squelch. Her words echoed through his mind and danced joyfully within his heart.

His kiss became a ravaging claim that left her no doubt how he felt. It was a savage brand, making her his, and she loved it. His hands moved over her body, burning wherever they touched, igniting fires in her that only he could put out.

The past, with all its questions and ugliness, ceased to exist, and tomorrow became a promise of sunshine.

Hart felt his body harden with the need of her. Pangs of hungry desire consumed him, filled every fiber of him with a craving so intense it threatened to destroy him if not satisfied.

Her hands slid through his hair.

His hands slid over her body, under her blouse, cupped her breasts, burned through her flesh.

He knew heaven was in his arms, and he never wanted to be anywhere else.

She had touched his soul, claimed it for her own and brought him a happiness he had never imagined possible.

He was lost to her forever, and it was the most wonderful feeling in the world.

Suzanne had no memory of how or when they climbed into the back of the Blackhawk sitting on the tarmac only a few yards from Hart's Cobra.

And it didn't matter.

Every cell of Suzanne's body begged for his touch, yearned to feel the fiery caress of his hands.

Their clothes were a barrier that gave way easily. His naked body melded to hers, hot flesh to hot flesh, communicating without words their need for each other, letting their desires run uncontrolled through their bodies, talking without words, loving freely.

Her hands explored him boldly as her need to know every inch of his body, every curve and line, pushed her wantonly on.

Hart nearly groaned as a shock of pleasure scorched through him, piercing stabs of ecstasy that raced through his body on a blinding, mindless course.

His tongue probed her mouth, feeding on the sweetness of her, as his senses fed on the exotic lure that she held over him.

She called his name when his hand slipped between her legs, whispered how much she loved him, needed him, wanted him.

They were words he suddenly realized he'd been waiting a lifetime to hear, feelings he'd been waiting a lifetime to feel.

The exquisite torture of need exploded within her at his intimate caresses, leaving her with no other awareness, no other thought than of him.

His hands framed her waist, lifted her above him, then brought her back down.

She felt herself fill with him, and a love deeper than anything she had ever dreamed.

Epilogue

Three Blackhawks hovered overhead.

Suzanne hurried toward the field, thankful she wasn't late, on this day of all days.

It had been a month since the night Brenner Trent, Kristen and Chief Carger had been arrested.

And it had been three weeks since her marriage to Hart Branson.

Suzanne smiled to herself as she made her way through the crowd mingling around the grandstand area, and remembered her wedding day. It had been a simple but beautiful ceremony in a small desert cathedral at dusk, and the beginning of a new life filled with more hope and happiness than she had ever imagined possible.

Clyde had come for the wedding, retrieved his ''baby'' and told Hart he absolutely hated him for taking away the best business partner he'd ever had. Contrary to his words, however, they had come to an arrangement that enabled them to keep their partnership intact, although long distance.

Suzanne would attend auctions and purchase estates, scouting out antiquities around Three Hills, Tucson, Bisbee and other small towns in southern Arizona, and send everything west to Clyde. Southwestern decor and pioneer furnishings were big in California now.

Her mother had come, too, cried all through the ceremony, warned Hart he'd better keep Suzanne happy, whispered to her that she had made the catch of the century and introduced them all to her new fiancé, soon-to-be husband number seven.

Suzanne pulled the brim of her large straw hat down a little farther in front, shading her face from the late-afternoon sun, and walked toward her seat in the parade field's grandstand.

She was a little later than she'd intended. Half the drills were already over. But her appointment in town had gone on a bit longer than she'd anticipated. The results, however, had been exactly what she'd been praying for.

General Walthorp's wife waved to her.

Suzanne smiled in return.

She saw the senator and his aide in the front row and nodded in acknowledgement. She knew what it meant to Hart that the senator had come.

The part of the proceedings she'd come to see were still several minutes away, so she stopped and chatted with some of the other wives. A moment later she glanced at her watch and excused herself. She'd told Hart she had a business appointment in town but would go to the ceremony as soon as possible and sit in the center grandstand, as near the first row as possible, and she wanted to be in her seat when he came out.

He'd said he would look for her, and she had to be there. Today of all days she had to be there.

The paratroopers who'd jumped from the Black-hawks gathered in front of the grandstand and saluted the generals sitting on a platform nearby. The boyish face of one of the paratroopers, so in contrast to the war-ready uniform he wore, caught Suzanne's eye and reminded her of another boyish-faced but very dangerous soldier she'd known.

The sound of the approaching Cobras suddenly filled the air.

Suzanne stood and smiled as she watched them descend.

They were black and deadly war birds, as lethal as anything imaginable, and they were one of the most beautiful sights she'd ever seen. Especially the one in the lead, the one with Ice written in small, white letters just below its canopy latch.

The breeze their spinning rotor blades sent across the grandstand as they descended was a welcome one that momentarily cut through the ninety-eight-degree heat of the day.

Suzanne felt her breast swell with pride as Hart climbed from his Cobra and walked toward the podium, Zack, Rand and several other corps members right behind him.

The investigation into Hart's background and his army personnel file, it was discovered, had been instigated by an overzealous clerk at the Pentagon. He'd wanted to make certain that every promotion recommendation that passed his desk had been thoroughly looked into and cleared. In total, ten investigations had taken place, causing nine men and one woman to wonder and worry if their careers were in serious jeopardy.

General Walthorp gave a speech about the corps, which he considered an invaluable asset to the army and the people of the United States, and called each man a hero in his own right.

"But today," he said, "we are here to honor the man who directly leads these heroes, Captain Hart Branson."

The general stepped away from the podium then and the entire Cobra Corps unit, standing at attention in front of the stage, saluted, then returned to standing at attention as Major Lewis stood and walked to the podium.

Suzanne felt her heart swell with pride as Hart was called onstage.

"Captain Branson," the major said as he pinned the gold oak leaf cluster to the epaulet on Hart's left shoulder. He stepped back then and handed Hart his promotion orders. "Congratulations, Major."

Lewis saluted then, as did every man in the corps.

As Hart left the podium, Suzanne left her seat and walked toward him.

Zack and Rand hurried over and slapped him on the back and congratulated him.

She quickly raised her camera and snapped a picture of the three of them, capturing the moment forever.

Zack and Rand had been at the house for dinner the previous evening. After they'd left, she'd told Hart that he couldn't ask for two better friends, and he'd surprised her by agreeing. That was when she knew he'd finally put the past and all its pain behind him.

"So how does it feel to be a major's wife?" Hart asked, drawing her into his arms and crushing her against his body.

"The same way it would feel if you were a private or president of the United States." She brushed his lips with hers, lingering for just a moment to savor the taste of him. "But—" she slipped her hand into his and pulled him away from the others "—I need to talk to you."

The seriousness of tone sent an instant jolt of alarm into his heart. "What's the matter?" It wasn't happening. It couldn't be. All his old fears suddenly rushed back over him, as if they'd never been gone.

"Hey, we're taking you to dinner in town to celebrate," Zack said. "Where are you two going?"

"We'll be right back," Suzanne said, tugging Hart away from the crowd.

"What's the matter, Suzanne?" Fear held his heart in its grip. He pulled her close, needing to feel her against him, wanting to hold her in his embrace so that whatever she had to say, she couldn't leave him.

Even though he knew she loved him, even though she'd married him and seemed happy, he knew now he'd never entirely banished the fear that someday she'd walk out of his life again.

Suzanne slipped her arms around his neck. "Hart, I know we were planning to go away for the weekend, but I don't—"

"What?" He frowned, his alarm growing. "Are you sick? Don't you feel well? What?"

She laughed. "I'm fine, sweetheart, really. I just

thought that maybe we should stay home and redecorate the guest bedroom.''

Relief flowed through him, but his frown changed to one of puzzlement. ''Redecorate the guest room? Why? Who's coming?''

Her smile turned wicked. ''I'll introduce you in about seven and a half months.''

''Seven and a half...?'' Hart stared at her, confused, then he understood. ''You don't mean...you aren't serious?''

They'd never talked about children, and suddenly Suzanne felt a chill of fear. What if he didn't want any? She tried to read his feelings in his eyes, but all she saw was disbelief. ''I am serious, Hart,'' she said softly. ''Is it okay? I mean, you do want—''

''Okay?'' He laughed. ''Are you kidding?'' He swung her off her feet and let out a whoop of joy that drew the attention of everyone on the parade field. But as swiftly as he'd swung her around, he stopped and lowered her back to the ground, alarm once again in his eyes. ''Oh, God, Suz, I'm sorry. Did I hurt you? Did I hurt the baby? Oh, damn, I—''

It was Suzanne's turn to laugh. ''I'm fine,'' she said. ''We're fine. And we loved being swung around by you.''

Hart pulled her back to him and claimed her mouth with his, savoring the sweetness of his wife's lips and knowing that for as long as he lived he would be thankful she had picked him to love.

Suddenly Suzanne realized what the alarm in his eyes had really been all about. She touched a hand to his face. ''I love you, Hart Branson, with every fiber of my being and more than you will ever know, and I promise that will never change.''

Tears filled his eyes. ''Thank you,'' he said, heart-wrenching emotion turning his voice to little more than a husky whisper.

Then he let out another whoop of joy, and holding Suzanne to his side, he turned to the other corps members, who were still staring and smiling. ''Come on, guys, it's time for that dinner party. But now we have a hell of a lot more to celebrate than just my promotion.''

* * * * *

Meet 50 loving dads in

& BACHELORS USA
Take 4 FREE BOOKS,
Plus get a FREE GIFT!

abies & Bachelors USA is a heartwarming new collection of reissued ovels featuring 50 sexy heroes from every state who experience the ps and downs of fatherhood and find time for love all the same. All f the books, hand-picked by our editors, are outstanding romances y some of the world's bestselling authors, including Stella Bagwell, ristine Rolofson, Judith Arnold and Marie Ferrarella!

**Don't delay, order today! Call customer service at
1-800-873-8635.
Or
Clip this page and mail it to The Reader Service:**

In U.S.A.
P.O. Box 9049
Buffalo, NY
14269-9049

In CANADA
P.O. Box 616
Fort Erie, Ontario
L2A 5X3

ES! Please send me four FREE BOOKS and FREE GIFT along with the next four ovels on a 14-day free home preview. If I like the books and decide to keep them, I'll ay just $15.96* U.S. or $18.00* CAN., and there's no charge for shipping and andling. Otherwise, I'll keep the 4 FREE BOOKS and FREE GIFT and return the rest. I decide to continue, I'll receive six books each month—two of which are always ee—until I've received the entire collection. In other words, if I collect all 50 volumes, will have paid for 32 and received 18 absolutely free!

267 HCK 4534
467 HCK 4535

Jame	(Please Print)	
ddress		Apt. #
City	State/Prov.	Zip/Postal Code

* Terms and prices subject to change without notice.
Sales Tax applicable in N.Y. Canadian residents will be charged applicable provincial taxes and GST. All orders are subject to approval.

IRBAB01R   © 2000 Harlequin Enterprises Limited

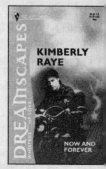

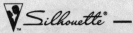

SILHOUETTE®
MAKES YOU
A STAR!

Look in the back pages of
all June Silhouette series books to find an
exciting new contest with fabulous prizes!
Available exclusively through Silhouette.

Don't miss it!

Silhouette®
Where love comes alive™

P.S. Watch for details on how you can meet
your favorite Silhouette author.

HARLEQUIN®

bestselling authors

Merline Lovelace
Deborah Simmons
Julia Justiss

*cordially invite you to enjoy three
brand-new stories of unexpected love*

The
Officer's
Bride

Available April 2001

HARLEQUIN®

Makes any time special ®

INTIMATE MOMENTS™

presents a riveting 12-book continuity series:

A Year of loving dangerously

Where passion rules and nothing is what it seems...

When dishonor threatens a top-secret agency, the brave men and women of SPEAR are prepared to risk it all as they put their lives—and their hearts—on the line.

Available May 2001:

CINDERELLA'S SECRET AGENT
by Ingrid Weaver

As a sharpshooter for the SPEAR agency, Del Rogers was determined to capture an arch villain named Simon. Love and family did not factor into his mission. *Until* he found the Cinderella of his dreams in the form of a pretty, pregnant waitress. Helping to deliver Maggie Rice's baby girl was all in a day's work. But keeping his heart neutral was an entirely different matter. Did this chivalrous secret agent dare indulge in fantasies of happily ever after?

*Available only from Silhouette Intimate Moments
at your favorite retail outlet.*

Where love comes alive™

Visit Silhouette at www.eHarlequin.com   SIMAYOLD12